*How to Not Fall for Your Best Friend, Book Three in the How to Not Fall series*



Author website: www.megeaston.com

**Nestled Hollow Romance**

*Coming Home to the Top of Main Street*

*Second Chance on the Corner of Main Street*

*Christmas at the End of Main Street*

*More than Friends in the Middle of Main Street*

*Love Again at the Heart of Main Street*

*More than Enemies on the Bridge of Main Street*

———

**Love Started romances**

*It Started with a Sunset*

*It Started with a Note*

*It Started with a Glance*

———

**Silver Leaf Falls romance**

*Coming Home to Silver Leaf Falls*

# HOW TO NOT FALL for YOUR BEST FRIEND

# HOW TO NOT FALL for YOUR BEST FRIEND

# MEG EASTON

# Contents

# CHAPTER 1

## Peyton

I HEFT my insulated bag of cold food items onto my dad's kitchen table. He bends to grab the bag of pantry items, but I slap his hand away. "Daddy. Your heart attack was barely two weeks ago. Obey your doctors."

"So I can't even lift a heavy bag for my little girl anymore?"

"Soon. Be patient."

I start unloading the ingredients in my bag onto the kitchen counter, and my dad helps. He pulls out the two small spaghetti squashes and a head of broccoli and then peeks into the bag at the rest of the produce. "Are you really going to make me eat this many vegetables?"

I smile. He complained a week ago, too, when I made him a bunch of heart-healthy meals right after he got out of the hospital. He never seems to complain after eating them, though. "You'll like what I do to them. Are you doing your exercises?"

He heaves a sigh once the bags are unloaded and sits down at the table. "Yes, but I need to get back to work. I think my doctor is being overly cautious. I've spent more time 'taking it easy' over the past two weeks than I have in the past ten years."

"Which is why you had the heart attack in the first place," I say as I start organizing the items on the counter.

My dad has always been a force. But since his heart attack, he sits less tall and doesn't seem larger than life quite as much.

"The firm needs me."

"They are handling things just fine on their own."

He lets out a long, slow breath. I can't see his legs under the table, but I can feel the slight tremor in the hardwood floor enough to know that his leg is bouncing. "I hate that people have to come to the house and help me. Flora shouldn't have to come. And I should be taking care of you, not the other way around."

When my dad went to the hospital and during those first few days after his surgery, my fear and worry were at the level of jumping out of an airplane. Now? I'm only at a bungee-jumping level.

"Your nurse will only have to come for another week or so. And if it helps, don't think of me coming to take care of you. Think of it as me just coming over for a regular old daddy-daughter chat."

He leans back in his chair, arms folded, a smile on his face. "Okay, then, Sugar Bug. Let's chat. How is work? Are you dating anyone new?"

I roll my eyes as I get out the pans I need. My dad takes

any opportunity he can to ask about my dating life. "Not dating anyone, but I do have a story about work." Since being home all day with not enough tasks to fill his time, he has turned into the best listener. And since I figure the term "laughter is the best medicine" hasn't been around so long for no reason, I save my most embarrassing stories for him.

Well, not *all* of my most embarrassing stories. I'm not going to tell him about how I tried on a fitted shirt at Sloan's a couple of days ago and forgot there was a back clasp when it came time to take it off. I got the shirt halfway up, and, arms above my head, I got stuck. The shirt trapped my arms tight against my head, leaving me unable to get the shirt up or down.

Seriously, I was as stuck as a flip-flop in wet sand. I had to leave the dressing room to search for someone to help free me. Which wasn't easy, since I had a shirt covering my face. So I bumped into an embarrassingly large number of things, including a carousel of bracelets that crashed to the ground, all while showing off my bra, before someone came running to find the source of the destruction and saved me.

I'll keep that story to myself.

As I wash the spaghetti squash, cut it in half, and then scoop out all the seeds, I say, "I got a brand new client this past week. Her name is Lavender, like the plant. Or the color, I guess. Anyway, she was a referral from another client, and we talked over the phone quite a bit and I created a menu for her."

I turn the heat on a cast iron skillet and start peeling and slivering enough garlic for the marinara sauce and the Thai turkey lettuce wraps I'm going to make next. "So I arrive at the woman's apartment building with all my stuff, get in the elevator, and push the button for the fourth floor.

"Right before the doors close, this good-looking guy, who was probably about my age, got in and smiled at me. Of course, I smiled back. He was all trim muscles and dressed nicely. Smelled great, too. It was a small elevator, so we were standing pretty close. Okay, actually, he was *really* good-looking."

My dad is smiling like he is expecting this story to involve flirty banter and the exchanging of phone numbers.

I pour some olive oil into the pan and then add the garlic, the whole tomatoes I crushed, and seasonings. "We were just passing the third floor, and the guy said, 'I'm going to miss you.'"

My dad's eyebrows shoot up.

"Right? But hey, who am I to judge if someone feels affection toward other people quickly? And it's not like I'm going to be rude."

"Obviously."

"So I said back, 'I'm going to miss you, too.' Because it was the polite thing to do, right? Then, the guy turned to face me fully with a weird expression on his face and pointed at his Bluetooth headphones. He was on a phone call! Which, he probably should've let his elevator mate know if he was going to be saying words that would make things uncomfortable if I responded. Then he said to the person on the phone, 'I love you, too. See you in a week.'"

"So at this point, I was sure my cheeks were flaming red because they felt like they were on fire. And that was when I noticed the wedding ring."

My dad is shaking his head and chuckling now.

"I probably should've noticed that earlier. But once I did notice, I thought, *Aww!* He and his wife are so sweet to each other! And I felt bad that they weren't going to see each other for a full week."

As I mix together the Romano cheese, cottage cheese, salt, pepper, and broccoli florets, I continue my story. "Then the doors opened for the fourth floor, we got off, and we both started walking down the hall in the same direction, which was kind of awkward. But not as awkward as when we both stopped in front of the *same apartment*!

"He pulled out his keys to unlock his door and gave me this look like I was some kind of crazy stalker who followed him home and was about to announce that I lived there now, too. But he still opened the door. And then he just looked at me as if he was about to pop some popcorn as he watched whatever shocking thing I was going to do next."

"I can't blame the guy," my dad says. "I'm wishing for a bowl of it in front of me right now just listening."

As the marinara simmers and the squash continues to cook in the microwave, I start adding the cilantro sauce ingredients to the blender for the lettuce wraps. "I was about to pull out my phone to verify that I got the right apartment when Lavender came to the door and said, 'Oh, you must be Peyton! Come in! And I see you've met my husband already.'

"At that point, the guy hadn't said one single word to me —not even 'Hi.' And all I'd said to him was 'I'll miss you, too.' But we both knew that he'd just told a woman that he loved her and would see her in a week. A woman who I now knew wasn't his wife! And then he wrapped his arms around Lavender and kissed her and told her he loved her."

My dad's eyes narrow. "What a dirt bag."

"That's what I was thinking, too. Lavender sat down at the table in front of her laptop because she was on a huge deadline. The guy gave me a nod and headed to some rooms behind the kitchen."

I put the blender on its base and turn it on, then pull the spaghetti squash halves out of the microwave. Once the blender finishes, I turn it off so we can talk again, and I start the ground turkey browning in a pan for the lettuce wraps. I use a fork to scrape up most of the squash strands before layering the cheeses and marinara sauce in them.

"So I get out my supplies and start preparing their meals. A few minutes later, the guy comes out wearing lounge pants and a t-shirt, goes over to Lavender, and starts massaging her shoulders. She closes her eyes and leans back into it. The whole time, all I could think about was how this guy was cheating on his wife and she didn't even know! And he was totally giving her a guilt massage. Because he was a dirty rotten cheater!"

"So, did you say something?"

"Not until I finished preparing the *I'm Sorry Your Husband Is Cheating on You* spinach rice to go with the honey mustard pork and made an *It's Too Bad He's Such a Jerk* spring minestrone soup and had it on the stove cooking.

"Then, when I was about to start the next meal, the guy left to go to the restroom. I gathered up my nerves, went around the kitchen island, sat down at the table next to Lavender, and told her that her husband was cheating on her. I was in such a cooking rush, probably because I was fueled by my indignation at the husband, that I might have just spit it out instead of easing her into the news. Of course, she was pretty alarmed and wanted to know how I knew. So I told her everything."

I stop telling my dad the story for a minute while I add the jalapeno, ginger, and lime juice and measure out the soy sauce—low sodium, of course. My dad just had a heart attack, after all—and add it to the Thai turkey lettuce wrap filling.

"And? I'm pretty sure my doctor would tell you not to keep me in suspense. I'm recovering from a heart attack, you know."

I smile at my dad's eagerness. It's why I like telling him stories so much. But I also like to make him good food, too, so sometimes that takes precedence. I start grilling tomatillo halves and some tilapia and then get out the cabbage for the fish tacos I'm making for our dinner tonight and start slicing it.

"Okay, so Lavender got up, grabbed her husband's phone, and opened the app to show the recent calls. Then she held it out for me to see and said, 'He was talking to his twin sister who's moving to Philadelphia. He's going on a business trip nearby next week and is going to help her get settled.'

"Dad, I was so embarrassed. I was entirely convinced he was cheating on her! And what kind of person would I be if I didn't tell her? The guy came out of the bathroom or wherever he was, caught the end of the conversation, and finally said his first words to me, which were, 'Maybe you shouldn't be so quick to assume things.' Which, okay, is totally true. But he did not say it in a nice way at all."

"Uh, oh. Did they fire you?"

I sigh and I shake my head. "No. That didn't happen until the spring minestrone soup on the stove started boiling over while we were talking. I had totally forgotten about it.

"In my rush from the table and around the island to get to it to pull it off the burner, I tripped over their dog, who apparently was also a ninja, because I didn't even know they had a dog and definitely hadn't heard him come into the room. He wasn't a very big dog, and in my attempt not to injure him—or me—I got way off balance and grabbed the only thing nearby, which just happened to be the edge of a decorative lacy doily-type thing on a lower counter, which brought her great-great-grandma's china bowl crashing to the tile floor."

"I'm so sorry, Sugar Bug."

"Yeah, I felt bad. But don't worry. When I left, the honey mustard pork was still in the crock pot and the spinach rice I made was still on the counter. After they ate it, they called me back and asked if I could please be their personal chef again."

"That's my girl."

"I just won't be cooking at their apartment because, apparently, the husband likes me about as much as a flat tire in a downpour, which is totally fine with me. About half of my clients have me cook at the inn because their house is chaotic, they feel like they have to super clean if I go to their house, or their kitchen is small. So it's no big deal. There's so much more space at the inn anyway."

As the two meals I made for him to eat later in the week cool, I cut up the softened tomatillos and toss them in a bowl with lime juice, red onion, pineapple, jalapeño, and pepper.

"Oh, I got something for you." My dad gets up and rifles through some papers he has on the counter. He smiles when he finds what he is looking for and holds a business card out to me.

I take the card and look closely at it, smiling. This one is for Pete and June's Dry Cleaning. I started collecting business cards when I was ten, and I have an entire wall in my childhood bedroom covered in them. Someday, when I have my own office, I hope to have enough to wallpaper the entire room with them. Business cards are the best because they're filled to the top with people's hopes and dreams, and I swear that looking at them powers my own hopes and dreams. "Thank you, Daddy." I give him a kiss on the cheek.

As the tortillas warm, my dad sets the table, and I move all of the dinner items to it.

After we sit, my dad holds my hand as he says grace, like he always does. And, like always, he blesses the food and the hands that prepared it. He always, always ends the prayer after saying that part. But this time, he pauses and then adds, "And please help Peyton to find a husband."

After we say amen, I just look at my dad. I don't know if I want to roll my eyes, chuckle, give him a gold star for practically doubling his normal length of prayer, or worry that he's more concerned about his health than he's letting on.

"What?" he says, trying to make his voice come out innocent but failing miserably. He pulls the tortillas toward him, then lifts the cloth and holds the container out to me. "I just don't want you to be alone."

A hand flies to my mouth. "Oh, exclamation points. You think you're going to die!"

He lets out a long breath. Then, apparently giving up on waiting for me to grab a tortilla, puts one on my plate for me and then takes one for himself. "I'm not going to die, Sugar Bug. Not until I'm too old to make it to the bathroom on my own. I just want you to have someone in your life."

I finally breathe again in relief, then put some cabbage on my tortilla and pass the dish to my dad. "I have people in my life. I have you, I have three amazing roommates, I have great clients, and I have Max."

"A best friend is not the same as a partner in life."

"I do date, Daddy. I just haven't found anyone recently that I'm interested in."

"If this heart attack has taught me anything, it's the importance of your relationships with the people in your life. And the most important relationship you can have is with a spouse. The person who will be there for you in thick and thin, through the good times and the bad, in times of health or heart attack. I want that for you."

"*Aww.*" I reach out and give my dad's hand a squeeze. "I want that for me, too." I grab the pineapple and tomatillo salsa and put some on my taco, then hand it to my dad and grab the fish.

He doesn't put the salsa on his taco, though—he just stares at me intently enough that I look up from where I am placing the fish chunks all perfectly on my taco.

"I'm serious about this."

"I know." My mom died eight years ago when I was eighteen, and since then, my dad has been married twice more. Neither of the two marriages lasted more than two years, and he isn't currently married. I like how happy my dad is when he's dating someone seriously or getting married to them. "Do you know what? You should date someone again, too! It's been four months since you and Meleah divorced. Maybe it's time."

"We're talking about you, Sugar Bug."

"You know, you're not exactly walking your talk." I wink to let him know that I'm not being rude—I'm just directing the conversation away from my non-existent dating life.

"I did walk my talk. With your mom. She was my everything, and I relished every moment we had together. I want that kind of relationship for you."

"Don't worry, Daddy. The right person for me will come along eventually. I'm sure of it."

"I only got nineteen-and-a-half years with your mom. If I'd known I'd only get that long, I wouldn't have waited until after law school and getting settled in my practice to find her. I would've dropped everything and searched five years sooner so I could've had that much longer with her."

I just stare into my dad's eyes, seeing in them the love he had for my mom, soaking in the feeling of her being in the room with us for a small moment. The truth is I want exactly what he wants for me. I want what my parents had. I want a man who will have that look in his eyes when he talks about me. I always have.

"Don't just sit around and wait—get out there and find him. Don't waste any of the years you could have together."

I don't sit around, waiting, so much as I stand around, waiting. I am always standing in the middle of the metaphorical dating street where I can be seen, willing to talk to anyone who comes out of their metaphorical houses and walks up to me.

But maybe he's right, and it's time to start going door-to-door, knocking. I've never done that. Do I even know how?

"Like I said, I don't plan on dying anytime soon. But the chances of having a second, larger, much more devastating heart attack after the first are pretty high. I want to see my little girl married before I go."

The thought of him not being around forever feels like a skewer to my stomach, so I drop the thought faster than a hot pan. His doctor already told me the statistics about second heart attacks. My dad is granite, though. It doesn't seem like anything will be able to take him down. He's been assuring me all along that he still has a lot to do on this planet and isn't anywhere close to leaving it.

But the fact that he actually said, out loud, that the chances of a second heart attack are there means he's worried. That, or he's just plenty serious about wanting me to find true love. Whatever the reason, I can tell by the look in his eyes that it's important to him.

I should take his advice. If it's something that's worrying him so much, maybe if I start seriously trying to find the perfect guy, it'll make him less likely to have a second heart attack. And I will do anything to lessen those odds.

It's not easy, but I work to replace the worried feeling in my gut with a determination to do all I can to help move along the process of finding my true love. I have absolutely no clue how I will accomplish that daunting task, but I suddenly find myself with oodles of willpower and hope that'll be enough.

"Don't you worry, Daddy. I'm going to go out and I'm going to find Mr. Perfectly Right, and then we're going to live happily ever after. You'll see. It'll pretty much be the best fairy tale ending ever."

He smiles, gives my hand a squeeze, then grabs the pineapple and tomatillo salsa and puts it on his taco. "That's my girl."

# CHAPTER 2
## *Max*

I WALK along the packed dirt of the McKenzie River trail in the Willamette National Forest, massive trees rising on both sides of me, my friends and co-workers Emilio and Leo right behind me. Ferns and bushes and various plants grow thick in the most vivid emerald greens, and down an incline at our right, the clear water of the McKenzie River moves around moss-covered rocks.

We've only seen two other hikers on the trail, both hiking in the opposite direction, so all we can hear are the sounds of insects buzzing and chirping, the breeze rustling the leaves and winding between the towering trees, and the river gurgling.

That and Leo swatting at every flying insect that nears him, cursing their very existence. It's as if the bugs know how much Leo hates them so they come near just to antagonize him.

"I don't think camping or hiking will ever feel right

without hearing you wishing death upon all the insects," I say.

Leo squawks and slaps his arm. Then he says, "I can't help it if I'm naturally the tastiest option here. I'm like a succulent prime rib dinner." He swats at his leg. "Is this why you guys brought me?"

"Yep," Emilio says, looking at a bridge that crosses the McKenzie River up ahead. "We know that Max and I are basically chopped liver, so they've got no reason to come after us when they've got you as an option."

Leo gives Emilio a friendly shove that nearly knocks him off the trail. But then the guy takes off his backpack, unzips one of his four trillion compartments, and pulls out a neon bracelet. He tosses it to Leo and says, "Put that on your wrist. Then they'll think you're about as tasty as apple cider vinegar and garlic."

Leo looks between the pink bracelet and me and Emilio like he's trying to decide if we're pranking him.

Leo was the last to join our camping product testing group, but he's been on enough campouts that he should know to trust Emilio. I clap him on the back. "Come on. You know Emilio is the king of helpful gadgets. He wouldn't haul something out here as a joke. Besides, that was made by us."

Leo turns the bracelet, probably trying to find the Blue Mountain Gear logo, before he looks satisfied.

We are coming up to a log bridge that spans the McKenzie River, but I gesture to a fallen tree trunk sitting in the water, green with moss, that covers nearly the entire distance. "What do you say we cross there? It'll give us a chance to try out the tread on these boots. If it fails, it'll give us a chance to see exactly how water-resistant they are." Besides, the log looks way more interesting than the bridge.

We make our way down to the river and start crossing on the fallen log, Emilio in front of me and Leo behind. And because Emilio is Emilio and Leo is Leo—and, to be honest, because I am me—we start trying to push each other off balance as we cross.

We've all developed pretty good balance, but Emilio bumps me hard and Leo follows it up with his own forceful nudge. I come close to giving the river a kiss. But I keep my balance (score one in the "good traction" column for the boots I'm testing) and even manage to put an arm in front and behind myself to give both men a simultaneous shove.

"How do you never go down?" Leo asks, giving me another shove.

Probably because the only time I ever really got to spend with my dad when I was a kid was on adventuring trips in the mountains. I'd wanted to impress him so badly back then that I tried to be good at every aspect of camping. Even walking across logs. "Because I was a pro long before you guys decided to give me so much practice at it."

Emilio nods at Leo. "You, me, let's make a goal to knock this guy off balance before the weekend is over."

They make the mistake, though, of reaching across me to give each other a fist bump to seal the deal. So I shove both of their arms toward the river and both men lose their balance. We are right at the edge of the river, so they only step into water that is a couple of inches deep, but hearing the splash as I step onto dry ground is rather satisfying.

I lead us the rest of the way up the trail until it opens to the view of Tamolitch Blue Pool. As we reach the edge of the cliff that stands seventy feet above the water, I hear Leo's low whistle. "Wow. That's...Wow. You guys said the water was super blue, but wow. That's blue."

"We have the best job in the world," I say, and the men on either side of me just nod in agreement. Scenes like this lake never cease to grab hold of me and make me feel like I've somehow won the Powerball of life. How I got lucky enough to be out here, testing outdoor products—many that I've had a hand in designing—and getting paid for it is unreal. My life is nearly perfect. I hope I never lose the sense of awe that comes from it.

"Are those the rocks at the bottom of the pond that we're seeing?"

I nod. "Pretty incredible, isn't it?" As far as payoffs at the end of a hike go, this one is a good one.

"What makes it so blue?"

"Hunter could tell you if he were here since he's the expert—"

"—on pretty much everything—" Emilio interrupts.

"—but it has something to do with the McKenzie River coming up out of the ground here after finding its way through volcanic layers."

Now that we aren't in the dense forest, I wonder if I can get enough of a cell signal to send a text to Peyton. She would love this view. If I have more than a bar of signal strength, I might even be able to send a picture. I pull out my phone, but there isn't so much as a hint of a shadow of a bar.

Leo steps a little closer and looks down. "It's so clear it kind of makes you want to jump in, doesn't it?"

"Don't jump," Emilio and I say at the same time.

"The pool is thirty feet deep," Emilio says, "but we're seventy feet above it. And that water is only thirty-seven degrees, so even if nothing went wrong with the jump, you'd enjoy plunging into that water about as much as Max, here, would like a life without camping. Or going a week without talking to Peyton."

I try to surreptitiously slide the phone back into my pocket, but the guys still notice. So I redirect their attention to the trail that is a steep decline down the left that leads to the other side of the pond, right near the surface of the water.

Like always, Leo gets out his camera and starts taking pictures—ones he will later send to us and will become the wallpaper on our computers and cell phones. The guy has an eye for art. It's nice to have our trips documented and to be able to relive the beauty of our surroundings later when we're all sitting in cubicles.

Leo motions with his camera to a boulder at the water's edge, just a couple of feet above the clear surface of the water. "Hop up there and give me your best 'King of the Mountain' pose."

So I leap onto it and stand with my feet apart, fists on my hips, looking up and off into the distance.

"I just got cell service," Emilio says, "and there's a text from Peyton. Catch."

Shock, elation, and worry as to what emergency made Peyton text Emilio when she couldn't reach me hits me at almost the same time Emilio's phone does. It smacks against my hand and I fumble it before it smacks my chest and bounces off. I juggle it some more, scrambling to grab it before it falls to the rock or into the water. It takes a leap toward the water, and I lunge for it and lose my balance.

I barely have time to register that fact before my whole body, backside first, plunges fully into the near-freezing water. As my head resurfaces, I gasp at the shock of it and try to get my limbs to kick into gear and get me out of there.

The faces of both Leo and Emilio appear over the boulder I was standing on a moment ago, and both men hold out a hand toward me. I wipe the water from my face and then reach for their hands.

"Okay, for the record," Emilio says, "I did not think that would actually work."

Leo shakes his head. "Me neither. You're a pro at not getting knocked off balance, after all."

As the two of them help to pull me out of the water and I manage to get both feet on the rock, my whole body shivers, and I try to keep my teeth from chattering. "I'm sorry I dropped your phone in the water."

Emilio chuckles, shaking his head as he leans down to grab something from the water. He holds it up. "I'm not stupid enough to chuck my phone at you like that. It's my tin of shower wipes. I didn't think you'd actually fall for it."

Not that I had enough time to see what the object was before reacting. I shiver again. When I came here last time with Hunter and Emilio, I washed my hands in the McKenzie, so I knew how cold it was. But it's nothing compared to my whole body experiencing it at the same time.

"Dude," Leo says, his focus on messing with his camera. "That was classic. I think I even got it on film."

"Send it to me," I say before turning my attention to Emilio. "Wait, so did Peyton actually text?"

Emilio shakes his head as he takes off his backpack and pulls a shirt from one of the compartments. "No. Man, you are so gone for this woman." He tosses me the shirt. "Change into that so you don't freeze. And ask her out already."

I take off my backpack, which is thankfully waterproof, and then remove my wet shirt before putting on Emilio's. Luckily the guy is always prepared because I hadn't brought an extra. Although if I'd known I was going for a swim, I'd have brought dry pants, too. "I'm not going to ask her out. We're just friends."

Both guys give me a look as we head back toward the trail.

"And do you *want* to just be friends?" Leo asks. "Because that look on your face every time you text her, or talk on the phone with her, or talk about her says otherwise."

I take a deep breath, grateful for the steepness of the trail and all the rocks and weeds slowing us down so I can think about how to answer. There are more than enough reasons why I want to take our relationship beyond being best friends.

But there are also many reasons that make it seem like the worst idea ever. Just one is that Peyton is looking for a husband, and I don't trust marriage even a little bit after growing up with my parents' dysfunctional marriage. Not that I'm going to share all of my reasons with the guys. To keep it simple, I just say, "She wants things out of a relationship that I can't give her."

I can't see Emilio's or Leo's faces to tell if they're rolling their eyes or nodding in understanding, and neither man says a word. So I add, "Besides, look what getting married did to Hunter. He only comes with us about a fourth of the time now, and I don't think I could survive conditions like that."

"Whatever, dude," Leo says. "It's your life."

———

Back at camp, once I'm dry and have spent enough time in front of the fire to feel like my bones are the temperature of a human instead of an ice pop, I get dinner on cooking. We're testing a grill basket that's replacing the one we've been selling. We tested it back at work, but this is the first time we're using it in the wild. From what I can tell, the clasp and handle we designed are far superior.

I give the veggies roasting in it a shake and then feel a buzz in my pocket. I pull out my phone to see a text from Peyton and smile.

Peyton: How is camping?

It looks like she sent it a couple of hours ago, so I don't know if she's still by her phone or not. I don't dare move an inch for fear I'll step out of whatever window of cell reception I happened to step into. Then I type my response.

Max: We haven't gotten attacked by any bears or had our food stolen by enterprising raccoons, so I'd say it's going pretty well.

Peyton: Raccoons don't steal food from Snow White. If they wanted your food, they would come right up to you and ask for it.

I smile, and not because my best friend just called me the name of a character who is a woman. I smile because she remembers I told her the guys gave me that nickname when they noticed how animals seemed to instinctively trust me. It was *months* ago when I told her.

I'm also smiling because I caught her when she can respond. It makes it feel like she's nearby. Like in the next camp over. I type my response.

Max: I'm already regretting telling you that piece of information.

The dots showing she's typing a response come up but then they disappear, and I glance at the top of my phone. Whatever wispy fog of cell service had graced our campsite has drifted away so I'm going to have to wait for that response.

"Catch!" Leo shouts while I'm still looking at my phone.

I don't even look up—I just let the pine cone Leo threw hit me in the shoulder and fall to the ground before I slide my phone back into my pocket. "You didn't think you could catch me off guard twice in the same day, did you?"

Leo shrugs. "No. Only Peyton can do that. I figured since you were texting her, I'd have my chance."

"You didn't know I was texting her."

Leo rolls his eyes like the notion of him not recognizing when I'm texting Peyton is ridiculous. I'm going to have to get better at not showing whatever is on my face when I text, talk to, or talk about her.

"You're off guard any time you're thinking of her. It's pretty much the only time you are, so it's easy to see."

I pick up the basket by the handle to turn the veggies over. As I lift it, the clasp opens, and all the vegetables I've been cooking spill into the fire. I grind my teeth as I watch half our dinner go up in flames, and then take a long, slow breath. "Looks like we've got some work to do on this clasp."

"Yeah…" Leo says, dragging out the word. "It was totally the clasp's fault. It had nothing to do with you being distracted by thoughts of Peyton."

# CHAPTER 3

## *Peyton*

I TURN from the road onto the curved drive of Hidden Inn after a really long day at a client's home where I cooked a week's worth of meals for a blended family of eight with very specific likes and dislikes and a handful of food allergies between them. They have two four-year-old boys—one from each parent's previous marriages—and they decided that the best place to have an all-out battle between teeny cars and plastic dinosaurs was around my feet and on my calves. But the pair were just so adorable that I couldn't bring myself to ask them to play elsewhere.

I'd been pouring all of my focus into creating the perfect roasted butternut squash risotto and somehow missed that they were quiet and no longer playing at my feet. That is until I turned around to grab the red pepper flakes and saw that the boys had gotten hold of my bag of gluten-free flour, dumped it out, and were using it as their car and dinosaur terrain. The two of them managed to get themselves covered in the white powder and look more like ghosts than preschoolers.

Luckily, my client knows her sons well enough that it didn't surprise her or make her blame me. What she didn't anticipate was how much they and I bonded, so as she was shepherding them off to the bath, she didn't manage to intercept them before they each gave me bear hugs.

I thought I'd done a decent job of getting the bulk of the flour off my jeans, but as I'm getting out of my seat, I can see that I'll have to take a trip to the car wash and vacuum it out soon.

Roman, my roommate Bex's fiancé, pulls into the curving driveway, parks behind me, and gets out as I walk up to the porch that wraps around the inn. I'm opening my mouth to ask how he's doing when the front door bursts open.

"I'm so glad you're both here," my roommate, Timini, says as she grabs our hands and pulls us inside.

"We don't have our roommate dinner tonight, do we?" I ask.

Timini shakes her head as she gestures for us to follow her into the kitchen and dining room area. "No, but Bex ordered pizza. And she has something to tell us that she's been keeping all buttoned-up about while we waited for you two."

I walk past all the smaller tables in the big space that guests used to eat breakfast at back when the place was run as an inn, but they are all covered in stacks of fabric, fabric cuts, scissors, pins, measuring tapes, patterns, and everything else Timini uses to create the pretty costumes she makes.

My roommate Addison and her husband, Ian, are seated at the big dining table just in front of the island counter. Bex stands beside the table, next to a stack of pizza boxes. Her face lights up when she sees Roman, and they meet each other halfway into the room and give each other the softest kiss. I can't wait for their wedding—the two of them are just as sweet as strawberry ice cream. They both walk to the table as Timini and I sit down.

Bex and Roman don't sit, though—they just stand looking at all of us and each other with excited faces.

"Holy guacamole," I say. "You finally found a house, didn't you?"

"Sort of," Bex says, looking at Roman.

Roman nods, not taking his eyes off Bex. "It's more of an 'on paper' kind of thing."

"I don't know what that means," Timini says.

"Well," Bex says, looking at all of us spread around the table, "we found the perfect piece of land about a mile down the road. We've decided to build."

I clap. "That's so exciting! I was worried you would end up moving far away since you weren't finding anything close, but that's the best news!"

"The only problem," Roman says, "is that the builder told us it'll be six to nine months before we can move in."

Bex nods. "Which brings us to what we wanted to talk to you all about. After the wedding, we are hoping to have Roman move in here with me while the house is being built. We already talked to Addison and Ian, since they own the inn, but Peyton and Timini, we want to know how you would feel about that. It's adding another person to the mix, and if you're not comfortable with that, we can move into Roman's apartment in Gresham, but we like it here and—"

Bex stops talking when the force of my hug hits her. I don't mean to throw so much energy into it, but I am just so excited that all of us are going to be staying together for longer. I am thrilled that Bex and Roman are getting married in just under four weeks. But that happy day also marked the end of an era. And now that era is going to keep going on.

"It looks like Peyton's vote is 'yes,'" Roman says.

"Of course it is," I say, and then give Roman a welcome hug.

"Timini?" Bex asks, and then bites her lip, waiting for the last roommate's response.

"My vote's a no."

My heart sinks. "Really?"

Timini snorts. "Of course, it's a yes. Who wouldn't want more love invading us at Hidden Inn?"

That is the best news I could've imagined hearing today. My roommates at Hidden Inn feel like family, and now it feels like our family is growing.

Halfway through eating the pizza, I say, "I want even more love invading us at Hidden Inn." Everyone looks at me like they aren't quite sure what I mean, so I explain. "You know how a health scare can make you reevaluate your life? Well, my dad's heart attack did that, and he told me how much he wanted me to get married soon. And do you know what? I want that, too."

Addison smiles wide. "I'm excited for you."

"You can't be excited about it yet because I don't know how to go about doing that."

Roman looks at everyone around the table. "So just propose to Max. *Bam*. Done."

"Ha ha," I say. "No—I need to find someone to date who is as perfect as Max is, and they need to be someone who would actually want to get married. I'm a planner, but I can't exactly plan my way into a happily ever after. I don't know what to do because my current plan isn't working."

"That plan where you wait until you stumble across someone while doing the normal things you do?" Bex says.

"Yep, that one. And then I date them for just long enough to tell if they're the one and start the process all over again when they aren't. And I don't happen across people often because single guys rarely hire personal chefs. If I keep doing what I've been doing, I'll be forty before I find someone. I want someone soon."

"So you need to speed things up," Timini confirms.

"Yes."

"Well," Addison says, "we could probably all set you up on dates with people we know."

Ian shakes his head. "If she goes on a few dates with each one, it'll take weeks before she gets to the next one. I bet we can think of a way to speed up the process."

"Like speed-dating?" Addison asks.

"No," I say. "I've gone to those things before. You can't tell enough about a person in a few minutes. You need at least a full date."

"And," Timini says, reaching to the middle of the table to grab a second slice of pizza, "if you go on a few dates in a row, it's easier to see what you like and don't like about the guys. What? That's not weird. Just ask Bex."

"The girl's got a point," Bex says. "In a strange way, it led me to Roman."

Addison taps a finger on her lips. "So, you need a lot of dates in a short amount of time."

"Yes," Timini says, "but you can't just *say* you'll go on a lot of dates. You need incentive or you'll give up when things don't go well. And it *will* get to a point when things don't go well. That's just the way it works."

"I already have incentive. I want a husband."

Timini shakes her head. "It's too far out. You need something more immediate."

"Oh!" Bex's eyes grow wide and she grins. "Maybe you can take those planning skills of yours and plan your way to a happily ever after. A *Find Peyton a Husband* plan. Make it a contest with someone else. Keep it short, like..." She looks around, her hands moving like she's trying to grab hold of something. "A week. See who can date the highest number of different people in seven days."

I sit up a little straighter. That might do it. Then, even if things don't go so well, it's not too long of a time frame. I can handle anything for a week.

"And then, at the end of the week," Addison says, "you can ask the one you liked the best to be your date at Roman's and Bex's wedding."

"Oh, this is perfect!" I say. Then I turn to Timini. "Do it with me. We can be in competition with each other, and it'll be fun. Plus, we'll each get a date for the wedding."

Timini snorts. "No. No way am I going up against the Queen of Enthusiasm in a contest."

I look at my roommates for help talking Timini into it, but Bex and Addison both hold up their hands.

"If I were single," Addison says, "I wouldn't have gone up against you, either."

"Same," Bex says.

Roman and Ian share a look that I can't quite interpret, and then a smile spreads slowly across Roman's face and he says, "Ask Max."

Max? I'm not so sure about asking him. I kind of sort of fell for him about a year ago, before I found out that he wasn't interested in me that way. It was tough, but I found a way to stomp out my feelings for him. If the two of us are competing, that might make me think about him dating more, which could make those feelings resurface.

But Max really does love any kind of competition. He will likely not only agree but push me to get so many more dates than I would on my own. He could be the key to the *Find Peyton a Husband* plan actually succeeding.

All I have to do is not fall for my best friend. That's it. Succeed, and I will be well on my way to getting a date for the wedding, finding a husband, and making my dad happy.

---

We are all still in the kitchen when I hear the sound of Max's car, and I go to the front door to greet him. I open it right as he reaches it, looking all manly in his snug jeans, hiking boots, and a t-shirt that hugs his chest perfectly. "You're back!"

"I just wanted to stop by on my way home and say hi."

I sniff as he steps past me into the lobby of the inn. "I smell campfire, but you look way too clean to not have been home to shower yet."

He gets the cutest look on his face. He ducks his head and his brows come together just a bit, almost like he's embarrassed about something, but one corner of his mouth curls up like he thinks something is humorous. "That's because I took a bath in the cleanest spring water there is."

"Are you hungry? We have some pizza, and I have a plan."

"A pizza plan?"

"No. Something even better."

I lead him into the kitchen and let him eat first because he's probably starving, even though I am dying to talk to him about the competition. About halfway through his second piece, he turns to me. "So what's this plan?"

I clap my hands together. "I was talking with my dad while you were gone, and I realized just how badly I want love in my life. You know, like Addison and Ian or Bex and Roman have. And I've decided I am done waiting for it to come along—I'm ready to go out and grab it myself."

Max is giving me a look, but I don't know what it means. "So this is where your plan comes in?" he asks.

"Yes. Well, we all came up with it together, and it's a competition. I know how much you like challenges, so I'm hoping you'll be my competition buddy. Anyway, the contest is about which of us can go on the most dates in a single week, and each date has to be with a different person.

"Date nights don't have to just be Fridays or Saturdays—we could go on dates every single night of the week. Lunch dates, even, if we wanted. And I figured we could fit a lot of dates in on the weekends. Like a breakfast date, a lunch one, an afternoon one, an evening one—we can even do a dessert date on the same night as a dinner date. Or a breakfast date before work. It doesn't have to be expensive dates, either. They can be walks in the park, or watching the sunset, or whatever."

Max just leans back in his chair, his pizza sitting on his plate like he's forgotten about it.

"So we were thinking," I continue, "you and I could find the dates this week, go on the dates next week, and then whichever date we liked the best, we'll ask them to be our dates for Bex and Roman's wedding two weeks after that. Because we can both bring a plus one."

"That's…a lot of dating," Max says.

"Doesn't it sound so fun? We can even help each other get dates! And we can ask everyone we know to set us up with people. And we can ask people out that we already know, or get a dating app this week and meet some new people. So what do you think? By the end of next week, maybe I'll actually find someone to marry, and I know you don't want to get married but you like to date and you might find someone you really want to keep dating."

"Did you say that all with a single breath?" Roman asks, looking impressed.

He shouldn't be so impressed, though. I shake my head

and hold up two fingers, but keep my eyes on Max. He seems like he's really thinking strongly about it, which probably means he's going to say yes. "I know you're used to winning, like, every single thing always, but don't just assume this is going to be easy. I plan to win. I'm going to be the toughest competitor that you've ever competed against."

"I don't know, Peyton."

I'm confused. Max lives for competitions. Normally, he would be smack-talking right now about how he's going to win by a mile. And he seems to like dating. "Oh! Of course! We need a prize for the winner." That must be why he isn't fully on board. "Um…" I look around at my roommates and soon-to-be roommate.

"I know," Bex says. "How about whoever loses has to sing karaoke?"

My face falls. I'm not good at that at all, so I'm going to have to make sure I don't lose.

Max looks at the others for a long moment, then his eyes find mine. "You seem really excited about this. Okay, I'm in."

"Yes!" Now that I have a competitor, I'm going to stick to this. The excitement for the next week is building up inside me to higher and higher levels the more I talk about it. "It is going to be the greatest week ever. You'll see. By the time Bex and Roman's wedding comes around, you're going to be so happy you agreed to do this competition with me."

"I'm sure I will."

He seems…unsure of himself, maybe? Almost nervous. Not his always-confident self. I've never won a single challenge against him before, so this face on him is new. Maybe he knows I'm going to win. Probably because *I* know I will win. "Don't worry. I'll be your wingman and help you find as many dates as you'd like."

"Thanks."

"Aww," Timini says. "Look at you two. You're going to go on a million dates and find the perfect one, and then all of you will have love."

"You're going to find love, too," I say. "We can help."

"Maybe you should get a dating app," Addison tells her.

Timini shakes her head. "I'm terrible at those things. You've all seen some of the guys I've dated—I always pick the pretty ones that turn out to be the wrong ones. I need a way to find someone to date without seeing their face. Like a blind date, only we find each other and talk a lot and find out if we're compatible before looks ever enter the picture. Then maybe I wouldn't always choose so poorly."

Bex's hand finds Roman's. "Your company should make an app like that."

"We should. Everyone deserves to find love." And then he gives Bex a kiss.

And it reminds me of what my dad said about relationships and how the most important relationship is with a spouse. I gasp and my hands fly to my mouth as the most wonderful, perfect idea flies into my mind. "Oh my life, Max. We should set our parents up with each other. My dad deserves love again and heaven knows that your mom deserves the love she never really got to have ever. It would be so perfect if they started dating each other."

"Set up our parents? Really?"

"Wouldn't it be so great?"

Max looks as uncomfortable as a cat wearing a bulldog costume.

"Max, it's not like I'm saying you should go on a double date with them. But think of how great it would be if they dated and things did work out between them. Then we wouldn't be just best friends—we would practically be brother and sister. I know you said you love me like a sister, but wouldn't it be so fun to actually be siblings?"

He stands up, and I search his face, trying to see if he's in a hurry, or upset, or just plain bored, but it doesn't give me any clues. "We have enough dates we need to set each other up on. I think we should just focus on that instead of setting up our parents right now."

"True," I say. "You're right—it can wait. Right now, we need to focus on this competition that I'm going to win."

I know enough about Max's competitive nature to know that the more I smack talk, the more committed he becomes to winning. Not that I'm good at smack talk. I wonder if there's some class or online course or YouTube video that could help me. In the meantime, I'm not going to let the fact that I'm bad at it stop me from doing it. Because this competition is a little bit scary and feels kind of huge if I'm being honest. And if Max is all-in on trying to win, it's going to make it that much easier for me to be all-in, too.

He gives me a smile but it looks tired, and it reminds me that he's on his way home from a camping trip. "I don't know, Abernathy. You're going to have to find a way to go on a lot of dates if you're going to beat me."

Max always uses my last name when he smack-talks. Which is fine, but then it makes me feel like I should use his last name, too. But since his last name is the same as my first name, it really just makes me feel like I'm talking about myself in the third person. So, instead, I always go for his middle name. "Bring it on, Augustus. I'm not afraid of a little competition." There. That sounded like decent smack talk. Score one for Peyton.

"I will definitely bring my A-game." Max glances at all of my roommates and then hitches his thumb over his shoulder. "Okay, I should probably go home to shower and unpack."

He says goodbye to me, and as he walks out of the kitchen and I hear the front door close, I feel the excitement for what lies ahead bubbling up inside me. I turn back to my roommates who are all looking at me with such a varied mix of expressions that I can't take it all in. "You guys will help set me up with dates, too, right?"

They all nod, and Timini says, "Of course. What are friends for?"

# CHAPTER 4
## *Max*

HUNTER TURNS the shoe dryer around in his hand. "It worked well, then, huh?"

The two of us are in the design cave, the area that is part computer lab and part showcase of some of the great items our team has designed.

I nod. "Like a charm. The inside of my boots were dry in no time after I fell into the lake. I'm sure we can make it smaller, though. I don't think it should have to be this bulky."

The two of us switch between physically picking up the piece of equipment we designed and turning to the big design computer screen in front of us, studying it, brainstorming ways to make it even better.

Hunter spent Monday through Thursday in our Hillsboro office working with the marketing team, so today is the first time I've seen my best guy friend since the camping trip that he missed. Emilio and Leo are great, but not the ones I'd ever go to for relationship advice. Hunter and I have been friends since before I even knew Peyton, so he knows our entire history. I've been dying to talk to him about her, but it's more of an in-person thing than a phone call thing.

"What if we make the length adjustable," Hunter says, then draws a circle around the middle of the shoe dryer on the screen, "and have this part collapse in and pull out? We'd have to make a little more space around the fan, but the overall bulk would be less."

"Good idea. And I was thinking we could alter the angle of the fan—" I use the mouse to move that element of the design "—and it might cut down on the space it takes. It would probably be enough to compensate for the collapsible section."

Hunter takes the mouse to make some changes, and I let him. I've got too much on my mind to focus on details. "So, um, Peyton decided that she wants to get married."

Hunter's attention jerks to me. "To you?"

"Okay, you don't have to look so shocked. But no, genius, not to me. Just, in general, she's ready to get married."

"You kind of knew that already."

"True. But she's ready to speed up the process." Peyton's my best friend—I want her to be happy. That doesn't mean I'm in love with the idea of her finding someone to spend her life with who isn't me. Imagining her married and moving forward with her life and leaving me behind has been playing over and over in my mind ever since she dropped that bomb on Sunday, and it's all making me a little crazy.

Hunter turns back to the screen, making adjustments to our design. "How is she planning to speed it up?"

I turn and lean against the design table, my arms folded. "A competition with me, actually. She wants us to see who can go on the highest number of dates—with a different person each time—in one week, and then we each take our favorite date to our friends Bex and Roman's wedding."

Hunter's still looking at the screen, but I can see the smile spreading across his face. "Stakes?"

"Karaoke for the loser."

This time, Hunter laughs. He even lets go of the mouse and turns in my direction so all his focus can be on me.

"And she wants us to be each other's wingman. So not only am I going to have to be hearing about her dates, but I'll actually be setting her up on dates with guys I know."

"Oh, man. I don't think you could get much more friend-zoned than that. Not that you haven't spent the last year pretty solidly in the friend zone."

"Thanks. I'm feeling better already."

Hunter chuckles. "Is she setting you up on dates as well?"

I nod.

"Well, at least you'll get a lot of dates out of the deal."

I let out a grunt of frustration and turn to the design screen. Getting a few dates isn't worth nearly as much as it's costing me.

"Why don't you just tell her how you feel about her already?"

I stay focused on the design, tweaking and re-tweaking the angle of the fan but making no progress. "Because that's not fair to her. I can't tell her, knowing how important getting married and starting a family is to her, if I'm not willing to get married or start a family."

Besides, even if marriage is something I could ever even fathom being okay with, based on the genes I got from both of my parents, I'm not going to be good at it—the being a husband part or the being a dad part. Both of which are important to Peyton.

"Oh," I say, "and I almost forgot the other twist in the story. She wants to set my mom up on a date with her dad."

This time, Hunter's laughter is so loud that the clothing design team on the first floor probably hears him. I turn away from the screen and wait patiently as Hunter finishes laughing.

"So, wait," Hunter says. "You're telling me that she's hoping to make you two officially brother and sister? That time when she almost kissed you and you said you love her like a sister is just going to keep coming back to bite you over and over, isn't it?"

Worst mistake ever. Someday, when I die, they're going to engrave on my headstone *Here lies the guy who told the woman he loved that he loved her…like a sister.*

I had sensed a shift in our relationship a year ago but was still caught off guard when we found ourselves face-to-face on a porch swing, whispering to each other just inches apart. Then Peyton glanced at my lips and began to close the considerably short gap between us.

I had been so panicked at the thought of not being enough if our relationship morphed from platonic to roman-tic, and therefore possibly losing a relationship with the person in the world who was most important to me that I had turned into an idiot and uttered the words that would follow me everywhere like a lost puppy.

"Hunter, I don't need to tell you how much my mom and her dad cannot date each other."

"Yeah, you've definitely got to squash those plans. Does your mom even want to get married again? I don't know her well but I didn't get the vibe that she was the marrying type."

"She isn't."

"Okay, the way I see it, you've got three choices. One: get over your issues and decide to be the man Peyton wants."

I roll my eyes. Like that's something you can just do.

"Two: keep things the way they've been. You go on your dates, she goes on hers, and you just keep acting like you've been acting for the past year—or really, the past four—and hope that Peyton never moves on and stays single forever so she'll always be your best friend and the woman you wish you could share a life with but know you never will."

I grab my chest, jerking back like Hunter just stabbed me with a sword. "Ouch."

"Or three: try to win the challenge. Go on as many dates as you can next week. Give them your all. Who knows? Maybe you'll find someone to date who will help you get over Peyton once and for all."

I nod. I haven't really put enough into dating lately. Partly because I'm not dating to find happily ever after like most people are, and partly because a big chunk of my heart has a *Reserved for Peyton Abernathy* sign on it.

But maybe Hunter is right. Pouring my focus into dating

could help me change that. I don't want to think about Peyton dating other guys and have actually loved that she's been too busy lately to date much. If she starts dating a ton next week, it will be easier to keep my mind off her if I'm going on dates as well. It could help me keep her in the friend zone as effectively as she keeps me in the friend zone.

Then, as long as whatever guy Peyton finds is worthy of her, I can be all-in happy for her.

"Good plan," I say.

"Yeah?"

"Yeah. I think it's just what I need. So if you have anyone you want to line me up with, next week is the time."

Based on the smile that spreads across Hunter's face, he already has some ideas of people I could date who would be perfect for me. Fantastic.

# CHAPTER 5

## Peyton

MY FINAL DISH for the family I'm preparing meals for, lemon chicken and rice, is simmering on the stove in Hidden Inn's kitchen, and the rest is finishing cooling as I clean up the last of the pots, pans, mixing bowls, utensils, and other dishes I've dirtied.

"And your dinner date tonight," Timini says as she cuts a pattern out of a large swath of fabric that covers our big dining table, "that's the one who is Bex's friend?"

I shake my head. "The dinner date is with a guy one of my clients set me up with. His name is Tyler, and I'm headed straight there after I drop off these meals. After that, I'm having dessert and a walk in the park with Bex's friend. Cohen, I think."

I hurry to dry my hands, then pull up my calendar app on my phone to make sure. How embarrassing would it be to get the guy's name wrong? "No! Cohen is dessert tomorrow! Grant is tonight. He seems as nice as summer sunshine. I don't know much about Tyler. I'm going in pretty blind for that one."

I put my phone down and start drying and putting away the dishes.

All of my roommates own their own small businesses. Addison and Ian are gone most days at clients' homes or Ian is in his shop. Bex spends probably half of her workday here in the inn, and when she's home, she usually works in the gathering room. But Timini does most of her work in the big room that holds the kitchen, our big dining table, and the half-a-dozen round tables. So the two of us have shared a lot of heart-to-heart talks over the past several months.

Bex must've finished her workday because she comes into the kitchen, searching for food.

"The pasta salad in that bowl is extra if you want some."

"Oh, Peyton! You are seriously the best." She must be really hungry or really in the mood for pasta salad because she's eating her bowl of it like she has just been found after being stranded in the desert for days. Between bites, she says, "Your week of dates starts today, right?"

"Yep! I meet the first guy in an hour."

"Bex," Timini says, "help me convince Peyton that one of her dates this week should be Max."

"Totally." Bex takes another bite, then adds, "You two get along great. You should try dating."

"Are we talking about Max?" Addison says as she walks into the room. She must've just gotten home. "Because if we are, I agree."

I start putting the lids on each of the dishes I've made, adding labels with reheating instructions along with which side dishes go with which main dishes. "Right. We should date and then get married and live happily ever after." My roommates are so funny.

"Exactly!" Timini says with a big exhale, like she's glad I finally understand. But really, it's Timini who doesn't understand.

"It's not going to happen, Timini. You know that." I grab the insulated bags I carry food in and start adding the ice packs to their linings.

"Name an objection if it did happen," Bex says.

I push the bag to the side. "Okay, here's one. Max's last name is Peyton. So if we got married, my name would be Peyton Peyton. *Peyton Peyton!* My name cannot be Peyton Peyton."

Bex grins. "Oh, but then we could call you PeyPey."

"No," I say. "Not allowed." I pull the first stack of containers toward me and start placing them in the insulated bag.

"You don't have to take his last name," Timini says. "You can each keep your own."

Addison sinks into a seat at the dining table, looking like her day has been exhausting. "Or have him take yours. Max Abernathy has a great ring to it."

I shake my head. "I'm a traditionalist. I'm taking my husband's name no matter what."

"Peyton Peyton aside," Bex says, "you can't tell me you've never thought about dating him. Because I don't buy in a million years that you've never thought of him as more than just a friend."

"Oh, I've thought about it, alright," I say as I put the last of the cooled meals into the bag and zip it up. "About a year ago, I kid you not that it was all I could think about. Then, one night, in the middle of me thinking how much I wanted to date Max, there were eight of us at a friend's house, playing games. Between having that many people in a smallish space and using the oven nonstop for appetizers, it got hot. So I went outside to cool down, and Max came out, too.

"You know how when you're super-hot and you go into cooler weather, it feels great at first but then you start to shiver even though you're not all the way cooled off yet? Well, Max and I were sitting on our friend's porch swing, and when I shivered, he put his arm around me and pulled me in close.

"We were whisper-talking so near to each other, and then suddenly we were having a moment. I swear to you, he looked at my lips. Which made me look at his, of course, because that's what you do when someone looks at your lips. And then I realized just how badly I wanted to kiss him right then and there.

"So, I started leaning in close, waiting to see what he'd do, and he leaned in close, too. We were maybe an inch away from each other when he pulled back and said, 'You know I love you, right?' Which really was exactly what I wanted to hear in that moment. But then, right after, he added, 'I always will. You're like a sister to me.' He loves me *like a sister*. So obviously that was the end of that, because *ew*."

Bex takes the last bite of her pasta salad, then goes to the sink and starts washing the bowl and fork. "Maybe he doesn't still feel that way. Or maybe it was a smokescreen. Maybe he wasn't ready for a relationship at that time and his brain just dumped that out as a way to stop its progression without ruining the friendship."

I put the lid on the shallow pot on the stove and flip up the locks that will hold it in place before nestling it into the insulated bag that will keep the meal warm for my client's family to eat for dinner tonight. "If that was the case, he wouldn't have spent the past year acting like it was exactly what he meant." I zip up the bag. "Plus, he's gone a lot. Which isn't a huge deal, but sometimes I just really miss him."

"See?" Addison says. "That's proof that maybe there's something between you."

"I really missed Timini when she went to visit her family for a week a couple of months ago." Missing someone is proof that you like hanging out with them. Not that you want to marry them. "Why are you all pushing this so much?"

Timini stacks her cut fabric pieces on top of each other. "Because, hello, we've seen the two of you together."

"I do think he's pretty perfect," I say because Max totally is. He's such a great friend, he's so much fun to talk to, we get along so well, and we're good at looking out for each other. "And I love being around him. But," I add, before they can comment too much on it, "it just wouldn't work out. I already came to terms with that." Of course, accepting that something is never going to happen and still pining for him are two different things.

I look at all the food I just prepared. "I like cooking for people, and I love that I can make a living doing it. But I don't have huge aspirations like you all do. I don't have dreams of owning my own restaurant someday or of having a big catering business. I really just want to get married and have kids and have them stand on stools beside me in the kitchen, wearing cute little aprons, and teach them how to cook, too. I might want to make a kids' cookbook or have a cooking with kids blog or something like that, but mostly I just want to make meals for people so they can be happy and healthy and have time to eat it with their loved ones.

"The part about my future that makes me so excited is being a wife and a mom, and I want to do it in time for my dad to meet his grandkids. Being good at both is my greatest aspiration. But Max has told me so many times over the years how much he doesn't want to get married. Not just that he's not ready yet—that he doesn't want to get married *ever*. Or be a dad. Which is just crazy, because I think he'd be great at both."

"Do you know why he doesn't?" Addison asks.

"Yeah." I look around to make sure I've packed up everything I need, then let out a big breath, resting my arms on the cooler. "Mostly because his parents were Mr. and Mrs. Bicker McBickerson. So he grew up thinking marriage was a horrible thing that constantly annoyed people.

"He must've gotten over it a teeny bit, though, because at some point he met Laurel. This was before he and I became friends. Apparently, they had a lot of chemistry and things got pretty serious between the two of them. Like, I think Max might have actually been considering marriage.

"But I guess chemistry didn't really matter, because they got along about as great as Max's parents had, and, I don't know. I think that kind of broke whatever thread of desire for marriage Max had left, and no one could convince him otherwise now. Plus, Max's dad was absent pretty much all of his childhood, so he never had a good example of a dad, either. I think he worries he might be the same.

"Anyway, I'm not going to give up my biggest dream in life, so it doesn't matter how great Max is. Not wanting marriage and a family is a deal-breaker for me."

A year ago, I had wanted to have my cake and eat it, too. Since then, I've come to accept that I can't have both and that Max and I will only ever be friends who love each other like siblings.

Or possibly actual siblings, if I can get our parents to fall in love.

"I get it," Bex says. "I couldn't imagine being as in love with Roman as I am and not being able to marry him."

Addison nods. "I agree. I want you to have it all. The falling in love, the marriage, the family—all of it."

"Me, too," Timini says. "So go out there and find the one already!"

I smile and then gather them all into a hug. I glance at the clock on the wall. "Oh! I better get going, or I'm going to be late for my date!"

I put a strap for each bag over my shoulders, then heft both out to my car. All I have to do is drop them off at my client's house and head over to the restaurant to meet my first date of the week. It's Monday. By Sunday night, just over six days from now, I will hopefully have gone on enough dates to have found the man who will be my future. Someone who will be open to marriage. Who knows? Maybe I'll even find him tonight.

# CHAPTER 6
## *Max*

THROWING myself into dating is the perfect way to get my mind off Peyton. I'm ready for this. Excited, even. It has been a while since I've gotten myself this psyched up for a date. I'm even wearing my favorite button-down and the cologne that always gets me compliments.

Caroline, the woman I'm going on a date with tonight, is someone Leo set me up with. Leo started out in hiking equipment design, and he and Caroline worked together before she left to work for a rival company. So at least we'll have something in common to talk about right off the bat.

Traffic on the I-205 is worse than I anticipated, and it's putting me a little behind. I left myself a cushion of time for something like this—I hope it'll be enough.

As I turn down the street the restaurant is on, I think about how Peyton is going on her first date of the week right now, too. Actually, she planned two dates for tonight. I'll have to step up my game if I'm going to fit in enough dates this week to win our contest. I wonder if she's going to have as easy of a time talking with her dates as she does talking to me. It's a given that the guy is going to fall for her. Peyton is an easy woman to fall for. But is she going to fall for any of them?

I need to get my mind off her dates and back on my own. Am I going to have as easy of a time talking to my dates as I do talking to Peyton?

I'm hopeless. I can't even stop thinking about her when I'm purposely thinking about my own date. *Come on, Max. You can do better than this.*

Okay, what do I know about Caroline? She worked at Blue Mountain Gear, so she's probably a fan of the outdoors. That could be fun. And Leo seemed really enthusiastic about setting the two of us up because he thought we'd be a great fit. The more I think about the date, the more possibilities it feels like it holds.

I've managed to get myself excited enough about it that when the traffic light turns yellow, I actually consider speeding up and racing through the intersection. But I'm far enough back that it'll be red by the time I reach it, so I ease on the brake to slow down. As soon as my car slows, I hear screeching then a crunch right as I'm thrown forward. It takes my brain a second to process that I've actually been hit in the rear by another car.

A quick glance in my rearview mirror tells me that a woman drives the car behind me, and other than experiencing a bit of shock, she looks okay. The light is red, so I quickly call 9-1-1 through my car's Bluetooth and report the crash. As soon as the light turns green, I drive through the intersection and pull off to the side. Great. Not only is this going to be a huge inconvenience, but it's really going to make me late for my date.

We both get out of our cars to check out the damage. We weren't driving fast, but it still did a good amount of damage to her front end and my back end—a little more than just replacing a bumper for both of us.

The woman whirls on me. "What were you thinking, stopping in the middle of the road like that?" She motions at our damaged cars. "This is exactly why it's against traffic laws. When it's a straight road in a thirty-five mile-per-hour zone, people expect you to go at least thirty-five, not just stop!"

My eyebrows come together. "There was a traffic light. It had turned yellow."

"Which means you speed up!"

"No, it means you slow down, which I did." I want to laugh at the ridiculousness of it.

The woman looks at me like I'm stupid, then puts her hands on her hips and shifts her focus to the road ahead for a moment. "Listen, I'm running late for an appointment." She turns and walks back to her car. "Let's just exchange information and get on our way."

I stay right where I am. "No, we need to file a police report."

"That'll just take longer. We don't need one."

If this woman is going to claim she isn't at fault for the wreck, I definitely want a police report saying in writing that she is. There must be an officer in the area because she pulls up behind the woman with her lights on before the lady who wrecked into me even gets a paper and pen from her car. The woman lets out a defeated sigh and stands with one hand on her hip, tapping her foot impatiently for the officer to get out of her car.

The woman argues with the officer, too, about who is at fault. Seriously, does she think that'll work? Based on how long she pushes her point, she must.

"Ducks are yellow, right?" the officer says. "Next time you're driving and you're wondering what a yellow light means, imagine a mama duck and her little ducklings crossing the road. They go slow, not fast, just like you should do when you see yellow." She marks something down on her clipboard. "Oh, and remember to follow at a safe distance so you've got time to stop when needed."

When she asks for our information, the woman steps forward to give hers first. I'm in a hurry, too, but this woman seems extra stressed, so I'm fine letting her go first. She still has to wait until the officer finishes the paperwork, so it's not like it really matters.

I stand back to give her some space while she gives her information, and I just watch, wondering what she's so stressed out about getting to. She's wearing a red dress. Not a business-like dress—more casual and fun, which really doesn't fit with what is obviously her current state of mind.

The moment the officer finishes getting our information and gives each of us a copy, the woman grabs it out of the officer's hand, gets into her car, and speeds off.

I toss the accident report into my front seat, then walk to the back of my car. I run my hands over my face and look at my ruined bumper and dented trunk. I haven't been on a date in nearly three months, and this week is supposed to get me back into dating again and get my mind off Peyton. This is not how I want to start it all off. I pull out my phone and open the message from Leo with Caroline's phone number, then send her a quick text.

> Max: I apologize for being late. I'll be at the restaurant in 5 minutes.

Then I take a picture of the damage and include it in a text to Peyton.

> Max: I hope your first date is going better than mine.

She responds quickly.

> Peyton: Max! Are you okay? What happened?

> Max: Just a fender bender. It's all good. I actually haven't met my date yet. Wish me luck!

She responds with three four-leaf clover emojis. Then one with a grinning face with fingers crossed on both sides of it. I smile and put the phone into my pocket, get into my car, drive the last few blocks, and then find a parking space. As I get out of my car and walk up to the front doors of the restaurant, I take a deep breath and hold my shoulders back.

This week of dates might be Peyton's *Find a Husband* plan, but it's my *Stop Thinking of Peyton as More than a Friend* plan. Today is the first day of it, and I'm going to crush it.

My date has already checked in with the hostess, which is no big surprise since I'm so late. What *is* a surprise is who the hostess leads me to.

The woman in the not-business-like but casual and fun red dress looks up at me as we near, a look of hope and anticipation on her face—until she realizes who I am and the expression immediately changes to a scowl. "Are you following me?"

I turn to the hostess and give her a "thank you" nod.

"Giving the officer my contact information because of the wreck doesn't give you permission to stalk me."

I hold out my hand. "Hi. I'm Max Peyton. You must be Caroline. Leo has spoken very highly of you." I speak formally as if we haven't just met in unfortunate circumstances. Knowing her last name for my introduction would've made it that much better—I wish I had at least glanced at the police report to see it before I came in.

"No," Caroline says. "No, no, no. This cannot be happening."

I take a seat. "The night is young, and we really haven't gotten a chance to know each other yet. What do you say we pretend we are meeting for the first time and go from there? We can consider the wreck a memorable meet-cute. Who knows? Maybe someday we'll tell this story at a party and everyone will be roaring with laughter, including us."

"I have a dented front end to my car. I'll have to spend time working with the insurance adjuster, find a reputable shop, and then be without my car while they repair it. My insurance won't even cover a rental car while it's in the shop. Oh, and my insurance rates will probably rise, and it's all because of you."

"Wait. You still think it was my fault?"

"So, no. I don't think we'll be at a party someday, telling people about our 'memorable meet-cute.'"

"Even after the officer told you I wasn't at fault?"

Caroline stands and puts her purse strap on her shoulder. "You are the most inconsiderate man I've ever met, and I hope I never have the displeasure of meeting you again."

"Well," I say, even though she is already storming out of the restaurant and won't hear, "I guess this date is over, then." I pick up the menu and start looking it over.

My start to a week of dating hasn't gone nearly as smoothly as I had hoped. If nothing else, I should at least get good food out of it.

As I wait for the waiter to come, I can't help but wonder how Peyton's date is going.

# CHAPTER 7

## *Peyton*

AS I STAND in line at the host's podium, I glance at the dining area of The Stone Slab. It's a fun, trendy restaurant that I've never been to before. I'll have to compliment Tyler on choosing a good one.

For a moment, nerves bubble up inside me. I've texted Tyler a few times as we ironed out the details of the date but we haven't chatted much, so I really don't know him at all. I can somewhat guess what he looks like simply because he's the brother of my client who set the two of us up, but I haven't even seen a picture of him. It's okay, though, because I trust my client and she thinks we'd be a good match. This isn't nerves. This is excitement about the possibilities of what this week will bring.

When the couple in front of me walks away to take a seat in the lobby, I step up to the host. "Hello. I'm meeting someone—Tyler. Has he checked in yet?"

The host runs his pen down his list. "I have a Ty."

"That's him."

The guy nods and picks up a menu and a set of silverware wrapped in a napkin. "I'll take you to him."

My date is seated at a table with his back to the room, so I don't get a chance to see his face until I get close. He's cute. A little younger than I was expecting—he doesn't look like he could be over twenty-four. But he has a sweet face and pretty eyes. "Hi," I say, sitting down across from him. "I'm Peyton."

The look on his face surprises me. If I had to name it, I'd say alarm or confusion, and it makes me wonder what my client told him about me. But then his expression seems to morph into curiosity, so maybe I'm not what he expected but he's okay with it.

He gives a nod, still with that curious look on his face, and says, "Ty."

I look down at the plate of food in front of him. "You already ordered?" If I was late, it was by one minute, tops. How early did he arrive? And why would he order just because he got there early?

Ty crinkles his brow. "That's what I always do when I sit down at a restaurant and the waitress comes to take my order."

I don't say that it's customary to wait for all members of your party before you do. But it's fine. It's not like everyone has the same customs. And maybe he's just an awkward type of guy and felt weird not giving his order when the waitress came. Awkwardness is fine. It's kind of cute on him. I pick up the menu that the host placed in my spot.

"So," I say as I glance at my choices, "would you recommend I get the same dish that you chose? Or should I try my luck at something else?"

Ty looks down at his plate, fork hovering just above it. "I got the Pan-Seared Salmon Rice Bowl. It's good, but if you get it, I'd recommend asking for it without the green beans. They make it taste weird."

I find it on the menu. It also has carrots, zucchini, squash, and a roasted red pepper sauce. It actually sounds really good, and Ty's looks tasty. So when the waitress comes by to take my order, I say, "I'd like the Pan-Seared Salmon Rice Bowl without green beans, please."

Ty smiles and takes another bite of his.

Honestly, it's kind of weird sitting across from him while he's eating when I won't have my food for a while. But he seems content to just sit there and eat. "So, Ty, what do you do for a living?"

"I'm an advertising copywriter."

"Does that mean you have jingles stuck in your head all day long?"

"Hah. No. I mostly write product descriptions for gardening supplies and fertilizer."

"You sound really passionate about that." He doesn't, actually. He sounds a little like he loves it about as much as a trip to the eye doctor, but I'm hoping that asking will prompt him to say what he's passionate about.

Instead, he just shrugs. "How about you?"

I tell him about being a personal chef, which he hasn't heard of before, so I tell him I have clients who want home-cooked meals but can't fit cooking into their schedule, so I cook for them regularly. And I tell him about how some clients have busy times because of various things and use my services only as needed. If nothing else, it fills the awkward time while I'm waiting for my food since he doesn't seem interested in filling it with anything else.

Eventually, my food comes—thank heavens—and I have something to do other than try to carry the conversation.

My cell phone text alert sounds—the text sound that I've set for Max. "I apologize—I have my phone on 'Do not disturb,' so that's an emergency bypass number." I pull the phone out of my purse and scrunch my brows at what little I see on the screen. I swipe to go into the text fully.

"Is everything okay?" Ty asks.

I shake my head. "My friend just got in a car accident."

"How bad?"

I pause a moment as I wait for Max's response to come in, then let out a relieved breath. "Just a fender bender. Everyone is okay." I quickly type a response back to him, and then put my phone back in my purse.

I'm only about four bites into eating my meal when Ty sets his fork down, apparently finished. Maybe he'll be chattier now. "So, Ty, where did you grow up?"

He eyes me. "You aren't trying to get password recovery information out of me, are you?"

I laugh. "If you could include your mother's maiden name in your story, that would be great. Oh, and your first pet's name, please." Then I take my fifth bite of dinner.

I'm glad when Ty laughs because, honestly, I wasn't sure if my comment would make him more at ease or convince him that I'm a spy trying to infiltrate his life.

"I grew up along the southern Oregon coast, then went to

Portland State. I got a job as an intern my senior year at the company I work at now and then just stayed after I graduated because there was really no reason to leave, you know? Well, except for the fact that it's boring, but I guess most jobs are."

"I don't know about most..."

The waitress comes by just then and sets the bill down next to Ty. The woman is about to walk off, but then Ty says, "Hang on a second." He gets out his wallet, pulls out a few bills, puts them in the folder, and hands it to the woman.

Then, to my utter bafflement, he turns to me and says, "It was really nice meeting you. Enjoy the rest of your meal." He then stands up, dabs at his mouth with his napkin, sets it on his plate, and walks away.

I notice a few moments later that I've been staring with my mouth open at the spot where I last saw him before he rounded the corner to the lobby. What just happened?

The waitress comes to my table and starts clearing away Ty's dishes because she doesn't want them to be in my way. So now I'm just sitting in the restaurant, all alone, looking like I'm here by myself. At least if the waitress had left Ty's plate and glass, it would've looked like my date had gone to the restroom or something.

I don't want to bug Max during his date, but I have to send him a text about this. Hopefully, he won't actually look at it until his date is over. I pull out my phone and slide open the camera first, adjusting it until I get my hardly touched meal and the empty spot across from me in the shot. When I open my phone, I'm still in the text with Max, so I attach the picture and type, *This is how my date is going. How's yours?*

His response comes less than a minute later. It's a picture of his meal at a different restaurant with a different background, but one thing is the same: the spot across from him is empty. His text reads, *About the same as yours*, with the zany face emoji next to it.

> Peyton: Oh, no! Did she never show up?

> Max: She showed up. I'm pretty sure she wished she hadn't, though.

> Peyton: [frowny face emoji] Want to talk?

As I wait for his response, I notice that I missed other texts while my phone was in *Do Not Disturb* mode. A few from my roommate chat… one from my dad… Oh! And one from Tyler. I tap that one first.

> Tyler: Hi, Peyton.

> Tyler: My boss dropped a huge project on me right as I was heading out the door and said it was important enough that none of us could leave if we valued our jobs. (Great boss, right? HA HA.) I am so sorry to cancel on you. I hope I caught you before you got to the restaurant. Can we reschedule for later in the week?

I stare at the text for a full minute, trying to make sense of what I'm reading before I stare at the spot across from me, eyes wide. Who have I been eating with? I grab the waitress as she walks by.

"Excuse me, what can you tell me about the guy I was having dinner with?"

The waitress shrugs. "Nice enough guy. Good tipper. I've seen him in here a few times—always alone, always orders the same thing. He didn't say he was expecting anyone today, or I would've had a glass of water waiting for you."

As the waitress walks away, I bury my face in my hands where I can feel exactly how hot my cheeks are. So I walked into a restaurant, sat down with a stranger who was very much not expecting me, and tried to make small talk with him while he ate?

I take my hands off my face and fan myself with my cloth napkin. But my level of scorching embarrassment is at a fire-alarm level, and the napkin is a water-pressure-challenged garden hose.

Seriously, what are the chances of a guy named Ty sitting in this restaurant, eating alone, at exactly the same time that I'm supposed to meet a Tyler? The chances are about as good as Bex going a week without using a single sticky note or Timini not leaving dirty dishes in the sink.

A business coach I worked with when I first started *Home-Cooked Heaven* told me, "Start as you mean to go." I really, *really* hope that this start doesn't have anything to do with the way my week is going to go.

No, I decide, it's *not* how it's going to go. I'm going to stay focused on finding the perfect guy, so I'm going to attract the perfect guy. That's all there is to it.

# CHAPTER 8

## *Max*

AFTER PEYTON and I pick up our sandwiches—mine a pulled pork and hers a roasted chicken salad—I head out to the café's large outdoor patio with her to find a seat. Thankfully, it's a sunny day and not looking like it's going to rain anytime soon. After having dates every night for the past four days, it feels so right to just be with Peyton again.

As we sit down at our favorite table at this restaurant— one that's a bit away from the other tables so no one else can hear us—Peyton puts a hand on my forearm, which always causes a buzzing in my chest. She gives a slight nod toward a young couple sitting on the far side of the patio. "Let's voice-over that couple."

One of our favorite pastimes when we're somewhere good for people-watching is to make up fake conversations that couples are having when they're too far away for us to hear what their conversations actually are.

This couple is probably discussing how work has been so

far today or what their weekend plans are going to be. But the guy reaches his arm up to scratch his back, his elbow sticking out above his head. So I pretend to be the guy's voice, making sure to keep my voice low enough that only Peyton will hear. "How about I wear a harness and we attach a rope right here. Then we could just lower me down through the skylight and I could grab the key. It seems easier than just breaking into the back door of the place. And, added bonus, we wouldn't have to rely on your ninja skills."

The woman says something next that we can't hear, and Peyton pretends to be the woman's voice. She gasps, sounding offended. "How dare you dis that! I have incredible ninja skills."

The guy looks down just then, which is perfect. "Not with those shoes, you don't."

The woman looks down, too. They probably just saw an ant or something crawling across the outdoor patio, but it fits. "True," Peyton says for the woman. "And these are pretty fabulous shoes, so I wouldn't exactly want to go in without them."

Then the woman must've gotten something on her hands, because she looks at them, palms up, rubbing her thumbs across her fingers. "Maybe we should lower *me* through the skylight, though. I'm the one with sticky fingers —you've got fumble fingers. You might just drop the key into a vent or someplace equally irretrievable."

The guy looks at his hands, too, so I say, "Yeah, I do drop things a lot. Okay, we'll lower you in through the skylight."

When the woman says something else, Peyton says, "But

how, exactly, do we sneak onto the roof of the building without getting the cops called on us?"

Neither of the two says anything for a moment, so I use my narrator voice and say, "They both sit in silence for a moment, taking bites of their food, clearly thinking things through."

The woman is the next to speak, so Peyton says, "I know it'd be embarrassing, honey, but it might make everything easier if we just called the locksmith and admitted that neither of us grabbed the house key when we left for work this morning."

I laugh out loud. I love playing this game with Peyton. It's been five days since I last saw her. Plus, it's been a very taxing week, so it seems as if it's been even longer than that. After going without seeing her, my whole mind and body are soaking her in, making me feel more grounded and alive.

She bites her sandwich and I take a bite of mine while I take in how beautiful she looks in the sunshine. Her curls are soft and look like spun gold. She's going to find someone to date and probably get married to this week. How can she not? She's amazing, and she attracts amazing people to her. Am I going to forever lose my chance with her? The thought causes sharp pains in my stomach, right along with a yearning to be the kind of man that Peyton would want to be with—the kind of man I very much am not. "How many dates have you gone on?"

She's chewing, so she holds up her fingers in answer.

"Nine? You've gone on *nine dates*?! We've only been doing this for four days!"

She swallows and dabs her mouth with her napkin.

"Well, I've gone on two each night—Monday, Tuesday, Wednesday, and Thursday. I've been telling the first guy that I'm free from six to nine or so and the second that I'm free from nine until midnight. Then none of them expect the date to go longer. And I went on one lunch date. Why? How many have you gone on?"

"Four, if you don't count the one that first night where she left. One each night since then, plus a dessert date." I thought I was doing pretty good with four. It felt like a lot.

"I can see you are really dying to sing karaoke."

I rub my hands on my face. I completely forgot about the stakes.

"Max, why didn't you have me set you up with people? I know single women who I think you would like."

I haven't let her because it's weird to have the woman I've been in love with for the past year and a half set me up on blind dates. I don't want to say that, though, so I shrug. "The guys at work have been way too zealous on their own."

"Well, you better tell them to step it up, or I'm going to win."

I really want to win. It doesn't matter the contest—I have a drive to win. But winning this contest kind of seems pointless because my plan is failing epically. None of my dates are actually taking my mind off Peyton. In fact, dating like this is practically guaranteeing she'll be on my mind all the time. If I'm not comparing one of my dates to her, I'm wondering how hers are going and hoping any dates that go well aren't going to impact my relationship with her.

She seems so excited about this competition when all I

want to do is stop competing. Stop dating anyone who isn't her. Wish she would stop dating anyone who isn't me. I imagine how her face would fall if I backed out, and I know I can't do it. I need to stop thinking about it so much and just play to win.

"I have a present for you," I say, pulling my wallet out of my jeans. I open it and remove the three business cards I've collected since I last saw her and place them, one at a time, into her open palms.

The look of wonder on her face is probably what makes me always keep an eye out for any she might not already have. That, and the fact that whenever she gets a business card to add to her collection, she says she knows it's going to be a great day. And I kind of want her to associate good days with me in the same way I associate good days with her.

She smiles. "You really are the best, Max."

The look she's giving me makes my heart race and my pulse pound. Then she reaches out and runs her thumb just beside my lips, soft and caressing. It's all I can do not to lean into her touch. I'm not sure what expression I have on my face, but the expression on hers feels like it mirrors my feelings toward her. I want to reach up and cradle her soft hand in mine. I want to touch her face, to run my finger along her cheek. To skim a finger along her lips.

"Mustard," Peyton whispers as she wipes the thumb she's run alongside my mouth on her napkin.

I clear my throat, forcing myself out of the trance I've fallen under, then nod toward another table, hoping that my voice doesn't come out as husky as I fear it will. "Voice-over that mom and three kids."

She seems to have been in a bit of a trance herself because her eyes stay on mine for a long moment before she turns to look in the direction I nodded.

The family is at a picnic-style table, with two young brothers on one side and the mom and a little girl on the other. The two boys are bumping shoulders and pushing each other for sport.

Peyton carefully puts the business cards I've given her into her purse and then says in a voice meant to mimic that of the little girl, who's probably five, "Can I have some of your fries?"

"Mom, tell him to stop touching me," I say.

The older boy starts putting his hands in his brother's face at the perfect timing, so Peyton says in a boy's voice that, honestly, is kind of hilarious, "I'm not touching you. I'm not touching you."

"Stop it," I say, as the younger brother, "or I'll tell Mom about the moldy cake under your bed."

Peyton, in that funny older brother's voice again, says, "No you won't, or I'll tell her how all your socks actually got holes." Then, in the little girl's voice, she says, "Can I have your fries?"

"Kids," I say in my best impression of a mom, which isn't going to win any awards, "stop tattling."

The older boy flicks the younger brother's hair, messing it up. "Hey," Peyton says.

"I was just making it look better," I say as the hair-flicker.

When the older boy tries to flick the younger one's hair too, the boy slides off the bench and maneuvers out of his brother's reach. The older one keeps trying to mess up the younger one's hair, but the younger brother is fast. Peyton says, "How will you know I love you if I don't 'fix' your hair?"

While the two boys are bobbing and weaving in the small space next to their table, the little sister quietly slides off her bench, goes around to the boys' side of the table, and sits with her legs across the bench, taking up both spots. "You didn't call seats back," Peyton says, as the little girl, "so that means I get to eat all of your fries."

When the little girl actually starts eating her brothers' fries, both Peyton and I laugh.

She gives me a smile that could power the sun. "I think we did pretty good on that one, especially considering the fact that neither of us have siblings."

I drink in the look on her face. I could stare at it all day. But as much as I don't want to know how her dates have been going this week, a part of me has to know. So I proceed cautiously. "Tell me about one of your dates that was just kind of *meh*." Then I take a bite of my sandwich so my face won't give anything away.

"Well," Peyton says as she swirls the straw in her ice water, "I went out with this guy on Tuesday, I think, and we met at a game center. I got there first and just waited for him in the lobby. When he came in, he got a little excited to meet me and decided to go for a hug. But then his foot caught on the rug at the door, tripped, fell into me, and we both went all the way down.

"So then, this guy who I've only known for about four seconds is on top of me and trying to see if I'm okay while trying to hurry and get up and act like it wasn't awkward while apologizing and still trying to make a good impression."

I'm smiling on the outside and laughing on the inside. Man, that would've been embarrassing.

"All of that would've been fine. I mean, I've had my share of unfortunate tripping. I don't know if it was just because of how things started out or if this was his normal, but for us being at a place that had 'fun' in its name, it was a pretty boring date. We played arcade games, bowled, played ping pong—he somehow even made laser tag boring."

"That takes some skill. You've got to give him that."

"Okay, tell me about one of yours."

"All right. I'll tell you my most boring one. I with with a woman to a restaurant. She was fairly interesting, and the conversation during dinner went pretty well, which kind of made me not expect the rest of the date. She said her roommates were watching TV at their apartment and asked if I wanted to join them. So I did.

"We got to her place about eight-thirty, and her roommates were all watching some show they all watch together about health insurance problems that I'm pretty sure wins awards for its ability to help insomniacs fall asleep. So I'm trying to act interested and marvel at how different this woman was when it was just the two of us versus how she was with her roommates.

"Then, at nine on the dot, an alarm on her phone sounded, and right in the middle of the show, she said it was her bedtime, thanks for the lovely evening, I'll see you later."

"Why didn't she just end the date after the dinner?"

"I have no idea. But that was definitely one where I should've planned a second date for the evening."

"Seriously, Max, it's like you're not even trying to win."

Okay, I can't have her thinking that. I need to redirect. "Maybe I'll win for the most awkward date. Tell me yours."

"Only if we don't count the ones where you got in a wreck and I had dinner with an unsuspecting stranger."

"Deal."

"Mine would probably be… Oh. Got one. I went out with this guy on Monday night, right after my dinner with a stranger. He wanted to go bowling, so we went to the bowling alley, and I found out that we were actually bowling with seven—*seven!*—of his guy friends. Apparently, they're a tight-knit group, and the guy was terrible about knowing if he should go on a second date with a woman, so he relied on them to make the decision for him."

"And? Do you pass their test?"

"I don't know—they didn't loop me into that conversation. But when my date went up to the snack counter to get us sodas, one of the friends started hitting on me, so, well, I guess that meant his vote could've gone either way."

I laugh. "Okay, that one's pretty good. I still think I've got you beat, though, from my date yesterday. We went to play tennis at some courts near her home. Another couple— friends of hers—were supposed to go with us so we could play doubles. When I got to her house to pick her up, she said that her friends had to cancel. But she insists that we can only play tennis as doubles, so we double—I kid you not —with her parents."

Peyton laughs, and, suddenly, the whole awkward date

was worth it just to hear that laugh. "Tell me you have at least one good one, though."

I nod. "One was." She's the one who's most like Peyton, though, which just makes all the ways she isn't Peyton stand out. And that pretty much does the opposite of helping me get over wanting a romantic relationship with Peyton. "How about you?"

I asked the question, and now it's too late to take it back. Every part of me does not want to hear about a date that went well. I hope she'll be as vague with her answer as I was with mine.

"A couple went pretty well. I'll probably date them both again. One was Wednesday night. My date and I went to dinner and couldn't find a single thing in common. The chitchat was epically awful. I'm talking 'bringing up foot fungus during dinner' awful."

"This was your good date?"

"Shh. I'm not done. So we were getting close to finishing our meal when the waiter came over to refill my date's water, and he spilled it all down the guy's front. My date gasped, called the waiter an idiot, and then said he needed to leave, obviously. Then he left before even paying for his half of the meal."

"That's awful."

"Wait, it gets better. So, after the guy left, the waiter came over and apologized. Then he told me that when my date got up earlier to go to the restroom, he actually went to the waiter and paid him twenty dollars to spill the water on him so he could make an early exit."

Why anyone would ever want to get out of a date with Peyton early is beyond my comprehension.

"So my waiter said he took the twenty bucks because if the guy was that big of a jerk, then not only should he be out of the money and have water spilled on him, but that I should know he's a jerk."

"I still don't get how this was a good date. Other than the fact that you get to end it early."

"Because the waiter used the twenty bucks to pay for the guy's meal, comped my meal, and then said he was getting off in ten minutes and took me for ice cream. His name is David, and he's pretty great, actually."

I really don't want to keep hearing about any dates that go well because imagining another guy with her makes me realize exactly how much I'm not okay with that. I have to get the subject moved off of dates. "Voice-over that older couple over there."

As Peyton starts talking in a voice that's supposed to be the older woman's, telling the guy about how he's a super-hero for fixing her broken lamp, one thought keeps going through my mind. Why can't things just stay the way they are?

Because right now, with Peyton in my life, everything is perfect.

# CHAPTER 9

## *Peyton*

EVERYTHING IS ALMOST ready for our big roommate date night. I just slid a spinach artichoke dip into the oven, Bex and Addison are putting together some cute little antipasti bites, Timini is scooping the filling into stuffed mushrooms, and I'm threading marinated tortellini onto skewers with bite-sized mozzarella, peppers, tomatoes, and basil. My date for the night is Noah, someone Bex lined me up with, and I've had a great time chatting with him over text all week.

I breathe in the scent of all the appetizers cooking. Tonight is going to be fun.

"I love *How Much Do You Know*," Timini says. "I'm excited we are going to play it again."

Bex lets out a long breath. "Oh, I so need this tonight! These last two weeks of preparation before the wedding are going to be brutal. And I swear all we've been doing lately is work and wedding prep. A night of fun is a godsend."

"When will Roman be here?" I ask.

"Soon. He had something he's finishing up at work, and then he'll be here. When's Ian coming?"

"He's just showering, and then he'll be down."

I turn to Timini. "You've got a date, right?"

"Yep." She sets down the scoop she's using and pulls out her phone. "His name is Mason. Isn't he basically a Greek god?" She holds out her phone so we can all ooh and ahh over him. "And look at this." She swipes to the next picture, which is a full-body image of him leaning his shoulder against a wall, legs crossed at the ankle, looking off into the distance like he's a model.

"He's definitely a pretty one," Addison says.

The guy is super pretty, but he really doesn't have anything on Max.

"Yeah," Timini says, sighing as she looks at the picture again before putting the phone back into her pocket. "So he's probably either a jerk or not so intelligent. I'm basically a pro at picking the beautiful man who's a jerk. I need to get over that." "Well, you are an artist," Bex says. "So of course you're going to appreciate the beauty."

Timini laughs. "I just need to get better at recognizing the inner beauty, too."

"Oh," Addison says, "I forgot to tell you. I was next door at Ian's grandma's earlier and mentioned we were playing *How Much Do You Know*. She said they love that game. Apparently, Carol can cream anyone at it. Meera can't because she's the least observant person she knows. Although Meera did say that she might not actually be the least observant person because she isn't observant enough to notice if someone else is less observant. Anyway, they want to come. Is everyone okay with that?"

"Oh, of course," I say. Everyone else agrees, which of course they would—they all like our next-door grandmas. When Meera moved in with Shirley and Carol a month ago, I told them that we needed to get one more of their Origami Club ladies to move in so that my roommates and I would each have a grandma to ourselves.

I'd said it to be nice, but then immediately realized that the reason either of them moved in with Shirley was because their husband recently passed away and they didn't want to live alone. So I had basically accidentally wished someone else's husband would pass. Sometimes I shouldn't talk.

"Meera said she'll run the game and come up with questions," Addison says, "which works out perfectly because it'll keep the teams even. Oh, and Shirley and Carol said to come prepared to lose."

A text notification buzzes on my phone, so I wash and dry my hands, then pick up my phone and read the text.

"What is it?" Addison asks.

I sigh. "It's Noah. He says his sister just went into labor. Which is exciting! But she wasn't supposed to for a few more weeks, and he had already told her he'd watch her two other kids while she and his brother-in-law were at the hospital. So he's on his way to their house now."

I type a response to him, telling him not to worry about having to cancel, and that I hope everything goes well with the delivery. Then I put down the phone. "What am I supposed to do now? *How Much Do You Know* only works if you play it as couples."

"Text Max," Bex says.

"I just had lunch with him today—it sounded like he had a date already planned for tonight."

Bex keeps her eyes on the antipasti she's working on, probably so I won't see the smile she's trying to hide. "It wouldn't hurt to ask."

Do you know what? It wouldn't. I open Max's name in my texting app and ask if he has a date for tonight. Part of me is crossing my fingers that he'll be unexpectedly free, and part of me is actually kind of worried he will be. Especially after our lunch today. We shared a moment where I'm pretty sure my feelings for him were on full display.

Going on so many dates this week has made my old crush on him not only resurface but come back with extra force behind it, which I hadn't expected to happen at all. This week was supposed to be about finding a partner who *wasn't* Max.

For so long, I've done amazingly well at only seeing him as a friend. Like seriously, someone should put me on a stage and hand me a really heavy crystal trophy with *Managed to not have romantic feelings for her very incredible BFF* engraved on it because that has been a monumental feat.

This week has been filled with so many guys. Tonight would make number ten. True, some of them have been disaster dates, but some of the guys have actually been pretty fantastic. There are four so far that I would go on a second date with. And I have a breakfast date, a lunch date, an afternoon date, and an evening date tomorrow. I even have a date to go to church with a guy on Sunday morning. So fifteen dates this week. Going out with that many guys and having the potential of going out with several again gives me so many choices.

So why does it make every part of me want to be with the one guy I can't have a future with? My heart races until his text comes in.

Max: I did, but I canceled it.

Peyton: Why?

Max: We've been chatting over text and could both see there wasn't anything there, so a date was pointless.

Wow. With as competitive as Max is, I'm surprised he's willing to have one fewer date. He's going to have to squeeze in so many dates a day just to catch up.

Peyton: My date just canceled on me, and we were going to have a quad date with my roommates and play How Much Do You Know, which I need a partner for. Are you free? If you say yes, I'll even let you count it as one of your dates.

Max: How can I say no to that? I'll be right over.

A smile spreads across my face, and I do a happy dance.

Timini raises an eyebrow. "Peyton, do you ever wonder if the fact that you get so happy whenever you find out you're going to get to see Max might be a sign?"

I pause a moment, then decide to tell the truth. "Lately? Yes."

"What?" The word practically explodes out of Bex.

All three women close in.

"Are you saying you have feelings for Max?" Addison asks, looking at Bex and Timini before her eyes find mine again. "Like, outside-of-friendship feelings?"

"It's terrible, isn't it? Because my life goals and Max's life goals can't co-exist. So I shouldn't be doing a happy dance because he's coming. Having feelings for him just makes finding the right person to spend my life with so much more difficult. And I really want to find that someone soon because what if something happens to my dad? I want him to get to know his future son-in-law."

"Do you know if Max has feelings for you?"

I shake my head. "I don't know. Sometimes I wonder if he might. But do you know what? It's irrelevant because we already know that the two of us would never work as a couple."

It isn't long before everyone's dates arrive and we all move into the giant gathering room and start snacking on the appetizers. The chairs are in two straight lines facing each other, five on each side, and we all find our way over and sit down across from our partners for the game. I grin at Max as Meera hands each of us a stack of note cards and a Sharpie.

"Anyone want to predict who will win?" Meera asks.

"We will," Carol says with as much conviction as she'd use when saying the grass is green.

"I don't know," Addison says. "Ian and I are pretty in sync. We plan to win."

"You might want to change your plans," I say, "because Max and I have known each other longer than everyone but Carol and Shirley." Look at that! I just smack-talked. I'm so proud of myself.

"Okay," Meera says, standing at the head of the rows of chairs, right in the middle of the two rows. Then, motioning to my side, she says, "Ladies, write down your biggest pet peeve, but don't show it to anyone. Gentlemen and Carol, write down what you think your partner's biggest pet peeve is. You've got sixty seconds. And…go!"

Pet peeves aren't the easiest thing to think of, but I immediately come up with an answer and write it down. I wonder if Max will even think of it.

"Addison," Meera says, "what did you put?"

Addison holds up her card. "Unorganized office supplies."

"Oh, man!" Ian says, holding his card. "I thought for sure you would say bead collections!"

We've all heard Addison complain about beads enough that it's probably what I would've guessed, too.

"Bex?" Meera prompts.

"Road construction when I'm in a hurry," she says, holding up her card.

Roman holds up his. "I went with 'People who are impatient with waiters at your favorite restaurant.'"

They chuckle and share a smile that tells me there's more to the story.

"Peyton."

I hold my card out for everyone to see and say, "When people say, 'I don't mean to be rude, but…' Because they *do* mean to be rude. What they should be saying is 'I'm about to say something rude, but I don't want you to judge me harshly for it.'"

"And Max?"

His grin spreads all the way across his face as he holds up his card. "Also 'I don't mean to be rude, but…'"

I reach across the space between the two rows and give Max a high five.

"Next up, Timini," Meera says. "What have you got?"

"Too many rules," Timini says, holding up her card.

"Well, I didn't have a ton to go on," Mason says, "but I wrote *high heels* because women hate high heels."

Everyone laughs and nods. But in our heads, we're probably only laughing and not nodding, because Timini is currently wearing high heels and had been showing them off earlier, talking about how much she loves them.

Meera gestures to the end of the row. "Shirley?"

"I put 'unclear instructions on origami or recipes.'"

"Yes!" Carol shouts. "I wrote 'when a recipe doesn't say all the instructions.'"

As we play each round, I keep watching Max, trying to guess if he knows the answer to one of mine or trying to guess his answer when it's one of his. His face is the cutest when he's trying to guess my answer. He looks at me like he's trying to see right into my brain. His eyes squint a bit, and his mouth does this little twitch-up at the corner that makes me want to kiss it.

Oh my goodness. I can't be thinking like that!

An hour later, Meera announces, "And that's the end of round ten!" The older woman is happier and more alive than I've seen her since her husband passed away. I'm so glad Addison asked them to come. "Max and Peyton are tied with Shirley and Carol at nine points each."

Carol raises her hand. "Only because one of the questions was 'What is your favorite number,' and who talks about their favorite number, anyway? Well, other than Timini."

Timini laughs. She had a giant number one on hers, which all of us could have guessed. Except for Mason, obviously. Every other couple got theirs wrong.

"Hey, don't blame the game. Now you know what to talk to each other about. Okay, Addison and Ian have seven points. Bex and Roman have six. Timini and Mason are bringing up the rear with one point."

Timini and Mason got that point because the question was "What was the last song you heard," and we were all listening to the same music. Mason was somehow still surprised that Timini guessed correctly. With as off-the-wall as the rest of Mason's answers have been, I'm kind of surprised that he didn't put a different song down on his card.

"Addison has a prize for the winner," Meera says, "so I say we do a lightning round with Max and Peyton and Shirley and Carol to determine the winner. Five rounds, and whoever has the most points at the end is the winner. Max and Carol, write down a food you won't eat." She pauses until we have our answers written down. "Max?"

"Apricots, kiwis, peaches, or anything like that."

I grin. "I wrote, 'Anything furry. Animals are furry. Fruit shouldn't be.'"

"Point for the whipper-snappers! Carol?"

"Oatmeal, because what I thought was a raisin in mine when I was seven was actually a curled-up spider." She shudders.

"Shirley."

She holds up her card with pride. "Oatmeal, because of childhood trauma."

"Point for the oldie-locks!"

For the next three questions, Max and I stare hard at each other, trying to make sure we get them right. The tension is mounting, and I really want us to win. First thing I'd buy if I won the lottery? A blast chiller and I'd make near-instant ice cream. I've dreamed about it in Max's presence enough that it's a quick answer for him. His worst habit? Biting pens. Easy. First thing I'd save in a fire? My business card collection.

It hits me how remarkably in sync with each other we are. I know more about him than anyone else in the world, and he knows more about me than anyone does. We know the best and worst of each other, have lived through our highs and lows, and have been there for each other through the good and the bad. Our relationship is stronger for it. It had been a teeny little shelter made of a rope and a tarp when we first became friends, and because of how much we know and care for each other, it has grown into basically a fortress.

"And we still have a tie!" Meera calls out. "Okay, last question. You'll both write down your answer and what you think your partner's answer is. I beg one of you to get it wrong or we might have to rock, paper, scissors the winner. Okay, all four of you, write down what your biggest fear is on one card, then write what you think your partner's biggest fear is on the other one. Go!"

Mine is easy. It's making the wrong decision, especially when it's something big. That has always been my biggest fear, ever since I was little. Well, that and bugs. But mostly choosing wrong.

Max's biggest fear, though… He's the most fearless person I know. He climbs mountains, jumps off cliffs, paraglides, takes off on camping trips with only the supplies he can carry on his back, and goes white-water rafting, skiing, and mountain biking. He doesn't even flinch a tiny bit when there are bugs. I study his expression as I try to decide.

Time is almost out, so I quickly write down what I see the most in his face. *Missing out on an adventure.*

Although that doesn't feel quite right. Missing out on… on what? Meera calls time, so I can't change it now. Besides, it has to be an adventure. He lives for it.

"Okay, let's get your answers. Peyton, show your biggest fear first."

I hold up my card and say, "Making a wrong choice."

The expression on Max's face is disappointment, and he bites his lip. Then he grins and holds his card up. "Making a bad decision, or having a big decision to make."

"Yes!" I hold my breath as Meera asks Carol what her answer is.

Carol holds up a card that reads *Bunnies.*

Then Shirley holds up her card, which has *Bunnies* written on it.

"Bunnies?" I ask. "For real? Floppy, hoppy bunnies?"

Carol shudders. "I can't even look at a picture of them."

I've heard some strange things tonight. Like the fact that Mason's dream job is to be the person who designs the little round metal rivets that are at the edges of front pockets on jeans. But *bunnies*?

"Okay, Max," Meera says, "show us your biggest fear."

I bite my lip. We're still tied, so we have to win this one. I finally exhale when Max holds up a card that reads, *Missing a chance at something.*

I look at Meera, and she says, "Point for the younglings!"

That was close. Especially because when I look at Max, I can tell that there's more to his answer than what he wrote.

"Okay, Shirley, it all comes down to this. What's your biggest fear?"

Shirley holds up a card that reads *Not moving forward.* "I know that you can't keep things the way that they are— things can't ever remain the same. My biggest fear is not moving forward because that means I'm moving backward."

That is such a great sentiment! I look over at Max and see the strangest look on his face. I don't have enough time to figure out what it means before Carol says, "*That* was your answer? How can that be your answer?"

"What did you guess?" Shirley asks.

Carol holds up the card. "Being alone."

"That used to be my biggest fear back when Henry first got sick. But I have all of you now, so I don't even worry about it anymore."

"Well, I hope you know that getting over your fear cost us the game." Carol puts a hand on her hip, trying to look judgmental.

"Max!" I say, "We actually won!" I jump out of my seat and he jumps out of his, and we hug. I'm so excited I have trouble keeping my feet on the ground.

Suddenly, I realize how very close our faces are. How I can feel the tickle of his breath on my lips. See up close how beautiful his eyes look as he gazes into mine. How amazing it feels to have his arms wrapped around my waist, his hands warm and strong against my lower back. How perfect it feels to have my arms around his neck.

*He's your friend, not a date,* I remind myself. *And definitely not a boyfriend. Back away.* I pull back a friend-sized distance. Or what I guess that would be. It's as if I suddenly lost all sense of how far that actually is. I've spent the whole night ogling him and thinking about how great he is, and it's as if it has made me forget how to act around him.

A flash of confusion crosses Max's face, and I don't know if it's because I've gotten the distance wrong and am sending an unintended message, or if he just can't guess what's going through my mind. Honestly, I'm not so sure myself anymore.

# CHAPTER 10
## *Max*

I SHOULD'VE GONE on a date last night. And another this morning, especially since today is the last day of Peyton's challenge.

But on Friday night, things just felt different with Peyton. Possibly because we spent so much time being so focused on each other and on how deeply we know each other. But I kind of think that maybe it was something more. That Peyton was feeling it, too.

I keep my Saturday morning breakfast and bike ride date with the woman Hunter set me up with. The date goes fine. The woman is fun to talk to, and we're pretty evenly matched when it comes to bike riding. She just isn't Peyton.

And going along with Peyton's week of dating hasn't helped me keep my mind off her at all.

Is it even fair to the last two women I have dates lined up with to take their time when my heart isn't in it? Probably not. So when Emilio calls and says they're doing a last-minute overnight camping trip in the Mount Hood National Forest with everyone, including Hunter, and that we're going to hike to Ramona Falls, I don't turn it down—I just cancel my dates. I think what I need is a night of camping to clear my head. It always does the trick.

———

Okay, it did the trick a little too well. Last night, as I lay in my tent listening to the sounds of nature, my mind did clear. But a clear, open, uncluttered mind leaves a lot of space available to really think about things, and I really thought about things. This morning, I still am.

We adjust backpacks at the trailhead, make sure boot laces are tied, and take last-minute drinks of water.

"Are you sure you remember how to do this?" Emilio says, bumping his shoulder into Hunter. "We could help you out and give you some tips."

Hunter, the guy who probably spends two hours a day reading about outdoor activities.

"I'm sure Max could give you some tips on how to not fall into freezing lakes," Leo says.

"Actually," Hunter says, giving Emilio a playful shove, "the thing I've forgotten the most from my long absence is how to carry a backpack. You could help out by carrying it for me."

As we head down the dirt path, surrounded by firs and pines whose trunks tower ten, twenty, or even thirty feet toward the sky before their lowest branches spread out, I ask Hunter, "So, do you miss coming out here as often?"

Hunter looks at the trail in the distance. "Yes and no. I've gone camping with Tami a few times on the weekends that I haven't come with you guys, so I haven't been nearly as camping-starved as you think I have been. I'm just waiting for you all to get spouses so we can go on couples' camping trips."

"Yeah, I wouldn't hold your breath waiting for me on that," Leo says. He's by far the youngest of us. He's also the most impulsive, so I wouldn't put it past the guy to be the first to surprise everyone and get married.

As much as I plan to never get married, Hunter's statement plants an image of being married to Peyton and going camping with her. Is that irrational? An impossibility?

The trail is only a slight incline through this part, and Emilio and Leo run ahead like they're brothers who are racing to get to the end. This time, I don't even care about winning. My mind is full and I have questions for Hunter.

"Can I ask you something personal? You don't have to answer, but if you do, I need your answer to be real."

"Shoot."

"I've hung out with you and Tami plenty of times, and you two always seem to get along decently well. Is it always like that? You know, even when you're not around other people?"

"A lot of the time, yeah. I mean, we don't get along one hundred percent of the time, of course. We have disagreements and we can get on each other's nerves pretty well, but we work through that stuff. Our marriage is not at all like what your parents' marriage was like if that's what you're asking—we don't just pretend to get along when we're in public. I know it's a weird concept, Max, but we actually, truly, enjoy being around each other. We are each other's favorite person."

For a long time, I thought my parents' marriage was normal. It was pretty much the same as all my friends' parents' marriages, so it seemed like that was just the way things were. I'm coming to realize that a big part of me still believes that. I wasn't married or even engaged to Laurel, but that was how things were with her from the moment things started getting serious between us. Our relationship dragged me down so low.

But that kind of relationship isn't universal—some people's marriages are great. I get that now. But could *mine* be, if I ever decided to get married? Or, since I have my parents' genes, am I destined to have a marriage full of bickering up until the day it dissolves?

"Does Tami like camping?"

"Not as much as I do, but she likes it well enough to go with me once a month or so. It helps that I go to farmers' markets and antique stores with her just as often."

I wonder if Peyton would like camping or if my two passions would be forever separated. "You ever think about having kids?"

Hunter nods. And then, in a quieter voice that tells me he isn't willing to share the information with anyone else, even though Emilio and Leo are too far ahead to hear, he says, "We are trying right now, actually."

My eyebrows shoot up. I hadn't even guessed that Hunter and Tami were to that point yet. After a long moment, I ask, "Do you think you'll still be able to go adventuring once you have kids?"

Hunter shrugs a shoulder. "I don't know. I mean, yeah, when they're older. For those first handful of years, though, I have no idea. I don't think we'll really know until we experience it. But I do worry about that. Especially because I won't be as effective at my job if I don't go out and test things.

"And you worry that you might lose a part of yourself if you just quit going."

"Yeah."

We both walk in silence for several long minutes. It's possibly the most honest, raw thing I've ever said to Hunter, and I'm kind of surprised that I actually have. It's not something I would've been willing to say to any other male on the planet, but I've known Hunter for long enough and trust him enough that my fears found a voice.

Because the truth is, my fears of marriage go further than worrying how my own marriage might turn out anything like my parents', strong as that fear is. I love my life. I had gotten a pretty clear picture of what I wanted my life to be like by the time I was a sophomore in college, and then I made it happen. It's even better as a twenty-seven-year-old than I imagined it would be as a nineteen-year-old.

But I worry that with all the concessions I'd have to make if I got a partner in life, the life I created would disappear. And that life is so intricately tied to who I am. I would feel lost and adrift without it.

Emilio and Leo are far enough ahead that I can no longer see them on the winding trail. Or anyone else. As the trail takes a sharp turn to the right, though, I hear another group coming toward us, and within minutes, they come around the bend. It's a husband and wife, and they're each wearing a child-carrying hiking backpack. In the wife's backpack is a baby that's probably less than a year old, and the dad has a bigger child-carrying backpack, probably for the preschooler who's running alongside him.

The trail is narrow in this section, so Hunter and I move off into the undergrowth as the little family passes, and we both stare at them the whole time. There's something about seeing a married couple—with kids!—doing the exact same thing we're doing that strikes me pretty hard.

I don't know why it hasn't occurred to me before that following my dream might be possible with little kids. The logo on their backpacks is a Blue Mountain Gear one, after all. I know my company creates them—I've just never been in on those projects.

I look at Hunter and can see that the same realization has hit him. That it's possible to involve a family in his passion. As we hike around the same bend the family just came from, we see Emilio and Leo at the river crossing, trying to push each other off a log that runs across it.

"Date Peyton."

My attention flies to Hunter. "What?"

"Is Peyton everything you want?"

"Yes."

"She seems to like being around you pretty well, and with as much of a pain as you are to be around, that's impressive."

I laugh and give my friend a shove down the path toward the river.

"There is no world in which I can imagine the two of you getting along as poorly as your parents did. The only thing stopping you is your own stupid issues, right? So just...get over them."

"Oh, is that all?"

As I step over a fallen tree in the path, Hunter says, "Your job is basically getting over obstacles. So you're literally a pro at it."

Could I overcome my obstacles? Could a future with her be possible?

The four of us hike the rest of the way to the falls more or less together. Except for the last bit, where Leo runs ahead to be the first one there. When I reach the falls, I take a moment to soak in the feeling of standing near the base of the waterfall. The water isn't as deep here—or as cold—as the one at Tamolitch Blue Pool, but I still make sure not to stand on any rocks at the edge, especially since my mind is even more full of Peyton than it was on our last trip.

The trail to the side that leads to the top of the falls is steep and narrow, so of course we take it.

"Hey," Hunter says as we ascend the trail, grabbing hold of weeds, brush, and logs as we make our way up the steep incline, "what do you all think of Max inviting Peyton to one of our trips?"

I shoot a look back at Hunter, wondering what he's up to.

"Think about it, Max. She could come with friends so she won't feel like she's just going with a bunch of guys. We have plenty of tent options. Then she could see what she thinks of camping."

"I like it," Emilio says. Then, throwing me a look, adds, "It would give us a reason to make better food."

"Hey. Blame it on the cookware," I say. "That meal would've been a lot better if half of it hadn't fallen into the fire."

Maybe inviting Peyton to go camping is a good idea. It might help me to know if camping together might be something in our future. Maybe it would help calm my worries that my life as I know it would cease to exist, making me lose myself, if I got into a serious relationship.

Leo makes it to the top first and disappears behind some small trees. Emilio is right in front of me, I'm a few steps away from reaching the level area at the top when Leo comes back around the corner, screaming, "Bobcat!"

My eyes widen in shock. I barely have a moment to react before Leo and Emilio are both half-running, half-sliding down the path, and crash right into me. I manage to pitch to the side so the three of us won't go bowling into Hunter, and then I'm tumbling through the undergrowth at the side of the path.

The upside to descending so quickly down a non-path is there are more things to grab hold of on the way down than there are on the path. The downside is, that the non-trail is every bit as steep as the trail and has quite a few more obstacles. Like half-buried fallen tree trunks. Big rocks. Bushes.

I bump and bounce and tumble my way down and, when I finally come to a stop at the bottom of the hill that seems to go on forever, I land in a patch of poison oak, their three-leaved vines beneath me, beside me, and stretching over me like they want to pull me down and bury me in the world's itchiest hug.

Between the fall and the poison oak landing, I am definitely going to be feeling this later. I lie on the ground for a couple of seconds, trying to catch my breath, as I hear my friends scrambling down the mountainside toward me.

My body aches—dull in some places, sharp pains in others—and the poison oak already burns. Yet, still, the thought pops into my head that maybe I should wait for my rash to clear before asking Peyton to go camping.

# CHAPTER 11
## *Peyton*

"SO," Max's mom says, "I gave him a look that told him, 'If you steal this parking space from me, this face is going to haunt your dreams for the next seven years.' Then the guy motions that the parking space is all mine, and he drives off to find a different one."

"Eleanor, you are so funny!" I remove the chicken I've been browning in a pan on Max's mom's stove and put in the veggies for the chicken cacciatore I'm making for her.

"I tell you. You've got to know when to be fierce to make it in this world. And by 'when,' I mean 'all the time.'"

We both laugh, and I say, "I love hanging out with you. I wish we could do it more often." Max's mom is just so different from me and always gives the most impossible-to-pull-off advice. It's fun and gives me a glimpse into a world I've never experienced. Really, the woman does everything fiercely, including loving people. It's nice.

"Oh, you know you're welcome here anytime you want.

Especially if you're going to make something as divine as what you've got going in that pan."

My phone rings, so I put down the spatula and pick it up. Seeing Max's name on the phone causes my heart rate to quicken. I answer with, "Are you on your way back?" I miss him. Sure, he's only been gone a day, but it's been two since I last saw him. Should I really be missing him this much? That's probably a warning sign that I should focus more on relationships that might be destined for more than just friendship.

"Yep. Do you want to hang out tonight, or do you have other plans?"

"I'm at your mom's right now—you should stop by. I'm making chicken cacciatore."

"I, uh, haven't showered yet."

I mouth to Eleanor, *Can Max shower here?* She nods, so I say, "Your mom says to just shower here. That way you don't have to go home and then come all the way back."

"Okay, then. I'm actually only five minutes away."

And he really does show up in about five minutes. When I hear the front door open, I go to the foyer to say hi and then stop in my tracks. "Whoa. Max! I've never seen you this dirty before!" From his head to his toes, he's covered in dirt. Like every square inch of him.

He looks at his mom. "You're having second thoughts about saying yes to me showering here, aren't you?"

"I'm just trying to decide if I should have you go in the backyard so I can turn the sprinklers on you first."

He holds up an empty garbage bag. "Don't worry. I'll put my clothes straight into here, and I'll leave the bathroom as clean as I found it. I'm going to have to wear one of my spare sets of clothes I left here, though. Nothing in my pack is clean enough."

The meal is simmering on the stove, so I just sit at the table, talking and laughing with Max's mom about my dates. Then I take a deep breath and bring up something I've been worrying about. "I've gone out with fifteen guys, so that's fifteen times I had to decide if I should continue to date them or not. I'm afraid I'm making all the wrong choices. I'm just not good at decision-making."

"You decided to come over here today, didn't you? I'd say you're pretty good at making decisions."

I laugh.

"In all seriousness, though, I think you *are* good at decision-making. I've never seen anyone more suited to being a personal chef than you are. I see the joy it brings you, so that's proof you can make good decisions."

"But I didn't make that decision—my mom did." Eleanor looks confused, so I explain. "When I was seven, I was helping my mom cook dinner and told her how much I liked helping her. She said I would be a great personal chef someday. So, I started watching cooking shows and she put me in cooking classes.

"When I was eighteen and just starting culinary school, she passed away. Before she died, she told me not to give up on my dream. It's the one decision I've always been totally confident about because it's the one she made for me. And now she's gone, so she can't tell me what the right decision is on anything. Like who to date."

"Peyton, I think you're better at it than you realize. Just listen to your gut."

"But what if I think everything is exactly right with a guy, and then later I find out it isn't and it's too late to change my mind? I mean we are talking about a decision that has lifetime implications! It's kind of an important thing to get right. How are people supposed to choose a partner for life based on such limited information?"

Eleanor looks like she's going to say something, but then Max walks in. It must have been a while since he last checked his spare clothes inventory because he's wearing a pair of teal gym shorts with a blue shirt that looks about as wrong next to the teal as peanut butter and grapefruit.

He's also limping and walking like everything hurts. And now that he's clean, I can see that there's a red, bumpy rash on his neck, hands, and one ankle, and several bruises on his legs and arms that are just starting to form.

"Max!" I say, hurrying to him. "What happened to you?"

"Well, a bobcat attacked. Except it wasn't really a bobcat so much as it was a cute little furry yellow-bellied marmot. So mostly Leo attacked, and I got to take the scenic route down the hill and got up close and personal with some poison oak. There were good times to be had by all."

I help Max to a chair. By the way he sits down, it looks like he has injured everything possible to injure. "What can I do? What do you need?"

"I'm good. I just need to sit for a minute. By tomorrow, I'll be one hundred percent."

His mom snorts.

"Okay, not a hundred percent, but better."

I look him up and down. "That rash'll take a week or two to go away, and bruises like the one I can see by your knee are going to take more than a day."

Max raises a shoulder in a shrug. He's trying to be tough, but I can tell it hurts. I want to wrap him up in, well, something that will make him feel better. I don't even dare hug him for fear it will make things worse.

As I sit back down at the table, his mom says, "Peyton was just telling me about some of the crazy dates she's gone on this week. Did she tell you about the one where the guy fell asleep?"

Max looks rather amused. "She did not." He leans forward, putting an arm on the table, resting his chin on his fist to show he's interested in the story. But it must hurt because he immediately puts his hand back down. "Tell me to distract me from the pain."

So, even though it's getting weirder to tell Max about my dates, I tell the story again. "Well, to start off, he didn't tell me that they had a huge deadline at his work and that he'd only slept an hour or two each night all week. He did tell me that they had worked all through the night and that he'd been up for thirty-six hours straight, but that he hadn't wanted to cancel the date. He didn't tell me that, though, until we were in the middle of a walk in a park. We saw a bench and he veered toward it. I don't think he'd even fully sat down before he fell asleep. Right there on the bench with people all around and kids laughing and yelling."

"That sounds like the most interesting date ever," Max jokes.

"Oh, it was," his mom says. "Keep listening."

"Max, I'm telling you that I tried hard to wake this guy up, and he just wouldn't. So I tried calling Addison, since she was the one who set me up with him, hoping that she knew someone I could call. But she was in the middle of organizing someone's cinder block garage and had no cell reception at all. So then I tried again to get the guy to wake up so he could tell me who to call, but, as I found out, when your body shuts itself down from lack of sleep, it shuts it down very effectively.

"So, I pulled the guy's phone from of his pocket and was trying to get his face to unlock it so I see if one of his contacts said 'Mom' or something, but did you know that you can't unlock your phone if your eyes aren't open? Anyway, I was kind of panicking by that point because I didn't even know if the guy was okay or if he was having some kind of medical emergency, and there was no way I could haul him back to the car to drive him home. And believe me, I tried.

"Then the police showed up, which was pretty handy—I wish I would've thought to call them. So I heaved a big sigh of relief that I was going to have help, and then the officer said to me, 'We got reports that you killed a guy and are trying to break into his phone and haul the body off to hide it.'"

Max starts laughing. And I do, too, because looking back now, it *is* funny. At the time, it was more embarrassing and exhausting than funny.

"But then I explained everything, and did you know that on an iPhone, from the password screen, you can tap Medical ID and it will show you who their emergency contact is? Because I didn't. Anyway, the police were going to take me to the station because even though the guy was clearly alive, they worried that I poisoned him or something, since he would not wake up.

"But then the guy's emergency contact, who was his roommate, told the police that the guy had only slept something like ten hours total in the past week, and the officers decided that I wasn't a criminal mastermind—I was just the victim of an unfortunate blind date. Which, if you ask me, was pretty obvious. If I were a criminal mastermind, would I really put the guy to sleep in the middle of a park with people all around?"

Max is laughing in earnest now. "Your date makes mine seem like a walk in the park. You know, the kind of walk in the park where your date doesn't fall asleep halfway through."

"Since Peyton told hers," his mom says, "you have to tell one of yours."

"Okay, then. Mine was lined up by a friend of a friend, so we both went in blind. Her brothers decided they needed to make sure their sister wasn't going out with a creeper, so they went to the same movie and snuck into the seats right behind us.

"The whole time, they were kicking our chairs, throwing popcorn, shouting at the decisions the characters made—all of it. I found out that it was a test to see how I'd react. I guess I passed the test because they started leaning forward and whispering advice on how I could subtly put my arm around their sister and when. All with her right there, listening."

My cheeks heat up just hearing about it. "Was she so embarrassed?"

Max shakes his head. "She high-fived her brothers on the way out."

"So who won your contest?" Eleanor asks. "And what does the winner get?"

We haven't actually discussed the final numbers, so I look at Max.

He sighs. "Peyton won."

I clap my hands, I'm so happy. A win against Max is nearly impossible, but I've done it. "How many dates did you go on?"

"Not important. Mom, to answer your question, the loser has to sing karaoke."

Eleanor covers her mouth with her hand like she's trying to hold in a laugh. "In public?"

Max's eyes shoot to mine before going back to his mom's. "Either, I guess. We never said."

"Well," Eleanor says, "then I suggest you not do it at home or your neighbor will be knocking on your door, asking if you have a cat in need of medical attention."

I chuckle. Max never sings for me—or anyone. I can't wait.

"So did either of you find a date for Bex and Roman's wedding? That was the goal, right?"

"Well, part of the goal," I say. "My ultimate goal is to find a husband. Or at least to hurry along the process." I glance at Max because apparently I'm now thinking of him as more than a friend, and it's weird to talk about stuff like that around him. The look on his face is unreadable. "I think I've narrowed it down to three. I might go with David."

"The waiter?"

"Yeah. He's a software tester during the day, and he's waiting tables a few nights a week to help pay for his niece's heart surgery." I turn to Max. "Have you decided who you're going with?"

Max immediately fumbles, and it makes me wonder if he hasn't already figured out who. "Um, yeah. I went on a bike ride with a girl named Clara. She seemed nice, so I thought I'd ask her."

"It's hard to choose, isn't it?"

I thought the date thing was a great idea, that I would sail blissfully through it, find someone incredible, and sometime soon, I'd be engaged, then we'd get married and live blissfully ever after. But I'm at the very end of my week of dating, and I'm more confused than I ever was. Especially whenever I look at Max. And especially when I think of Max going to the wedding with Clara.

Eleanor gives a rare sweet smile. Not a teasing one or a patronizing one or a conspiratorial one. It's one full of love. "I'll just say that I think both of you will find who you're supposed to be with, and you'll know that person is right."

By the look on Eleanor's face, I can't tell if she's just wishing me good fortune in general or if she's thinking of Max and me together when she says it. I'm going to assume good fortune in general because the other is too big to wrap my head around.

"Aw, thank you," I say. "Speaking of finding who you're

supposed to be with, I was talking to my dad the other day, and I think he's ready to start dating again."

Max kicks my shoe with his under the table. I glance at him, expecting his expression to be apologetic for straightening his legs right into mine, but he's just looking at me with an intense face that I can't read.

"Anyway, so then I got thinking that you—"

Max hits his leg right into the table this time, shaking it, and causing him to wince in pain at the bruise that must be on whatever part of his leg hit the table. As he's wincing, he reaches up and starts scratching at the rash on his neck.

"I'll go get the calamine lotion," Eleanor says. "With a son like Max, I know to always keep it on hand. Oh, and I finished putting together a scrapbook for you, Max. I'll grab that, too."

As soon as she leaves the room, Max says, "Peyton! I thought we agreed not to set them up!"

Why did I even bring it up? Maybe because I'm having trouble shoving my feelings for Max down, and him being my brother seems like an effective way. I hadn't even realized that was what I was doing.

Sneaky subconscious.

Max lets out a big exhale. "My parents' marriage wasn't like your parents'. Unless they were performing for an audience of friends, mine bickered nonstop. I think the reason they went on so many vacations when I was a kid was because the only way they could almost get along was if they were somewhere exotic. They didn't like each other like your parents did. Do you really want your dad to be with someone who will bicker with him all the time?"

"You don't know they will bicker. Your parents probably did just because they weren't a good fit for each other. My dad was so happy when my mom was alive. I want that for him again."

"Peyton, your parents' marriage was a unicorn. Something rare that can't be duplicated. That's not how it works for other people."

"It *is* how it works for other people." I wish he understood that. "It just didn't for your parents. My dad is a nice guy, and your mom has been nice to him the few times they've met. I think she'll like him. Don't you want her to experience a marriage that is better than the one she had with your dad?"

And now I'm fighting for it. *What is wrong with me?*

Max runs his hands over his face, frustrated. "Can you— Will you at least just wait a while, like a month or two, before doing anything?"

Give in, Peyton. Just back away. You don't want to win this one. "Okay. I won't set them up."

I'm just going to have to come up with another way to keep my thoughts under control about having a romantic relationship with Max. Preferably before my subconscious brain starts making plans again without my consent.

# CHAPTER 12
## *Max*

I'M SITTING with Clara in the audience for Bex and Roman's wedding ceremony. Everything looks so nice. And Roman looks like the happiest man who has ever lived. It makes me actually imagine myself standing at the front of a crowd of my closest family and friends, about to be married to Peyton, looking every bit as thrilled. It surprises me how much the thought doesn't freak me out.

I turn as Peyton comes up the aisle with the other bridesmaids and groomsmen, arm-in-arm with one of Roman's friends, and then goes to stand at the front, facing the guests.

All seven of the bridesmaids are wearing dresses with the same slate blue fabric, but each in a style all their own. None of them stand out the way Peyton does, though, or look as amazing in that color. Hers is fitted to just past her hips before it flares, the silky fabric falling in perfect waves, showing off her incredible legs. I'm having the hardest time keeping my eyes off her.

The music changes, and then Bex comes in, escorted by her dad, and I go on imagining what it would be like if it was Peyton walking up that aisle, looking just as thrilled about our future together as Bex is looking about hers.

Bex and Roman have written their own vows, and I'm not ashamed to admit that I tear up a little. Peyton's eyes find mine, and the look she gives me makes my heart race and swell and maybe even melt a bit. I try to read her expression to guess if she is possibly picturing this happening with us like I am. It occupies all my attention.

Once the ceremony is over and it's time to head into the reception, I walk in with Clara. Peyton is right in front of me, practically floating. I know from watching her during the ceremony that she has loved every minute of it.

Clara reaches for my hand and gives it a squeeze, reminding me that Peyton and I aren't here with each other and that I shouldn't be imagining a life with Peyton when I have a date by my side. I shouldn't be thinking of her at all. Peyton's eyes immediately shift to David's, who she's walking hand-in-hand with, and she gives him a smile.

It's a clear reminder that things are the way they always are. I'm in love with Peyton, and she doesn't know. I'm just moving through life with her as a best friend and not as a partner.

"Look how beautiful everything is," Peyton says as she motions to all the fancy tables and place settings and chairs with bows tied around them. The big long table where Bex and Roman will sit, along with her four sisters, his two brothers, two groomsmen, and both of their parents, is long and at the top of the room, facing everyone. The rest of the tables are circular and go along the other three sides of the room, leaving the middle open for dancing. All of us find our way to the tables we're assigned to.

My table is at the top of the U, closest to the long bride and groom table. I find my and Clara's names at two of the place settings, pull Clara's chair out, and then tuck it in as she sits. Peyton is seated at the same table, directly across from me, which makes her the easiest to look at and the most difficult to speak to, especially in a room with the noise from so many people talking. And, of course, David is by her side.

Addison and Ian are seated to the left of my date, and Timini and a guy named Orion are to my right. I've only known the guy for an hour, but already he doesn't seem like Timini's type at all. Other than the fact that he is pretty and she seems to like the pretty ones.

I scratch the back of my neck, the very last of the poison oak rash looking like it's gone, thankfully, but not all the way over its itching. Especially when I'm wearing a collared shirt. I'm glad that the bruises and aching bones didn't take as long to heal.

As soon as we are all seated, Bex and Roman come into the room, waving to everyone and smiling like they aren't freaked out at all about having just gotten married.

"You know when I tie the knot," Orion says as the wait staff places salads in front of each of us, "I'm not going to worry about all this traditional stuff. In fact, I think I want to purposely do the opposite of tradition."

Kind of curious, but mostly looking to make conversation that will keep my mind off Peyton, I ask, "So, in regards to the meal, does 'opposite of tradition' mean something along the lines of serving breakfast instead of dinner, serving dessert first, or having the guests be the servers and the servers eat the meal?"

"Well," Orion says as he picks up his dessert fork and stabs a piece of lettuce in his salad, "I was thinking more like having it on the beach, and instead of tables, everyone just sitting on beach towels in the sand to eat, but I like the way you think."

Timini tries to hide her smile. Orion might not make it to another date after this one, but she is clearly fascinated by him. Actually, everyone seems to be a little bit.

"I want a flash mob at my wedding," Clara says. "But since those are usually a surprise to the bride and groom, it's the one thing you can't plan, which is too bad."

"Invite me," Orion says, "and I'll make sure you have one."

"Thank you," Clara says, seeming very touched by his offer, especially since they only met minutes ago. Then her expression turns unsure. Probably because she's imagining what kind of song for the flash mom he might consider the "opposite of tradition."

Movement from the dance floor catches my attention, and I look over to see three of Bex's young nieces, each smiling and carrying something in their hands, and it looks like their focus is on my table. While chatting with my table-mates, I keep glancing back at the girls, who are making their way closer, but only because they are doing a lot of nudging each other.

I'm surprised when they come straight over to me, and each of them places the things they have been holding—

which turn out to be rose petals—in a pile next to my plate. I've seen all three girls at the inn before, but I don't know their names.

"She thinks you're cute," one who looks about five years old blurts out, giving a little shove to a girl who is probably around seven.

"No, she does," the seven-year-old says, pointing to someone barely older than her.

The oldest smiles at me and says, "Actually, we all think you're cute."

The other two nod.

"And I think all three of you are beautiful," I say. "I like your matching dresses. Thank you so much for the rose petals."

The three girls giggle, and then flat-out run their way across the dance floor and back to their parents' tables.

"Aww," Peyton says, watching the little girls run. "Wasn't that the sweetest thing?"

"It was." Addison shifts her attention to the table where Bex and Roman are sitting, making moon eyes at each other. "I can't believe our little girl is all grown up."

Ian chuckles. "I can't believe Roman finally stopped caring what his dad thought."

"I can't believe two of us are married now," Peyton says.

"I can't believe more of you aren't," David says, which really just kind of irks me.

"I can't believe that's how you'd measure a woman's worth." I'm not sure David hears me, and I'm not sure I want him to.

"I can't believe they put cream in the dressing," Clara says next to me.

Orion looks over at the tables where Bex's sisters' husbands and kids are seated. "I can't believe they let all these kids come to the reception and run around everywhere."

"I can believe it," Timini says. "Bex wouldn't have had it any other way. Plus, they're sweet."

"Excuse me a moment," Clara says, and then gets up and walks away.

I give her a nod and then look back at Peyton and David. I know that what I'm feeling when I look at David is jealousy—I'm not so oblivious of my own emotions to not recognize it. What I've wished a million times over during the past two weeks is that I'd been willing to tell Peyton I wanted to come with her to the wedding before she asked David.

Actually, I wish that I'd confessed my feelings for her anytime in the past year. Or, if I'm going to go back in time with my wishing, I wish I'd been open to the possibility four years ago when we first met and became friends.

But now I'm here with Clara, on a second date after the first hasn't even been great, and she's here with David on a date that *does* seem to be going great.

After a few minutes of trying to focus on eating the grilled beef tenderloin with lobster risotto, mushrooms, and carrots that a server has placed in front of me, Clara sits back down and leans in close to me. "I'm…not doing so well. Do you think you can take me home?"

One look at her could've told me she isn't feeling well.

Which is crazy, because she looked fine just a few minutes ago. I hurry and put my napkin on the table. "Yeah, of course."

"Clara!" Timini says when she looks over. "Are you okay?"

"I just ate something I'm allergic to." She waves her hand. "I'll be fine."

My eyes meet Peyton's as I stand, and I see a sadness in them that I'm leaving. A longing for me to stay. My face probably mirrors hers. I give her a small smile and escort Clara out of the building, then run ahead to get my car which is finally back from the auto body shop, good as new, and drive it back to her.

"Do you need me to take you to the hospital? Or to an urgent care clinic?"

"No. I just need to go home."

I know I wouldn't be the most pleasant person to be around if I were sick, and I don't expect Clara to be, either. But I also don't expect her to be so mad at me for bringing her. And I think it's a bit much when she starts shouting curses at the chefs, the wait staff, the people who purchased the ingredients, Bex and Roman for choosing the menu, the dairy farmers who sold the cream, the cows who produced the milk, and everyone who attended the wedding for supporting such an atrocity.

She was such a calm, even person for our first date and the first half of this one. I never would've guessed she'd turn into someone capable of coming up with the vocabulary needed to swear up the storm she just unleashed.

Once we pull up to her apartment, I open the door for

her and help her out of the car. She looks miserable. "Can I come in and help? Or go get medicine? What do you need?" I feel helpless and am not quite sure what to even offer.

"I just want to suffer alone." She turns and puts a hand on my shoulder. I'm not proud of the fact that it makes me flinch like she might slap me. "You are a lovely man, Max, and I appreciate you for leaving your friend's wedding to get me home. But obviously, we can never go out again after this."

She turns and walks away, and I'm left feeling bad that she's so miserable from the date I've taken her on.

As I get back in my car and drive away, though, I glance at the clock. The night is still young—it isn't too late to go back to the wedding. Sure, Peyton will be with her date all night. But she's Peyton, so I feel pulled back to the event, anyway.

# CHAPTER 13

## *Peyton*

BEX'S WEDDING is magical and the most beautiful ceremony I've ever witnessed. Bex and Roman look amazing and so happy. Both the room with the ceremony and the reception room are fancy and pretty. The dinner is delicious. And now I'm dancing with David, having fun and feeling so elegant in my perfect dress.

So why has my mind spent so much of the night thinking about Max?

Probably because I don't get to see him so dressed up very often, and he looks so good in his suit. And probably because I'm having a harder and harder time viewing him as just a friend. Which is probably why I'm having such a difficult time watching him with Clara. Max and I haven't ever doubled on dates, so I'm not used to it. I might be a little bit jealous.

And I'm probably thinking about him so much simply because he's Max. Max just pulls people to him.

But Max left, the music is great, everyone is on their feet on the dance floor, and I'm dancing with a guy who has been a model of a perfect date all night long. So I put all of my focus on him and on enjoying the moment and not thinking about Max. And mostly succeeding.

Well, succeeding a good half of the time.

We are dancing to a song that is great for the swing, and David is an excellent dance partner. He twirls me out, and right before he twirls me back in, I swear the feel of the reception hall changes. As we dance, I try to look around to see what's different.

And then I see it. Max has come back to the reception. My heart feels like a balloon being blown up to bursting that he came back. Bex's little nieces must feel the shift in the room, too, because they immediately run over to him. And then he starts dancing with them and my heart melts into a big pile of goo.

David and I continue to do the swing—arms extended and then back together—and I do a pretty decent job of having all of my attention on him. Well, except for when I'm facing Max's direction and catch another glimpse of him doing the random silly dance moves the little girls are doing. He's such a good sport. At the end of the song, David drops me into a dip, and I smile up at him.

When he pulls me back up to standing, he meets my eyes and says, "Thank you for the dance." Then he glances toward the doors. "I think I'm going to go."

"What?" I study his face. "Already? But it's not over."

He gives me the sweetest smile and then touches a lock of hair that is resting on my shoulder. "I know. And I've had a wonderful time with you, but I pride myself on being a gentleman." I look at him, not making the connection between that and him leaving, so he nods at something behind me. "Your friend Max is now dateless, and he is in love with you, so I'm going to take a step back."

I jerk my head back in confusion. "What? Max? No—we're just friends."

David shakes his head. "Not to him. And by the way you light up whenever he's in the room, I think the feeling is mutual. I've been watching all night, and I think you should go explore that."

I turn to glance at Max, who must sense we are talking about him from across the dance floor because even though he has three little girls pulling on his hands, his eyes are on mine.

When I look back at David, I say, "I'm sorry I've been a terrible date." Because if I've been focusing on Max enough for David to notice, I very much have been.

He shakes his head. "You've been a phenomenal date. I like you, Peyton. If things between the two of us went some-where, I'd be thrilled. But not while you're in love with your best friend."

Am I in love with Max? A voice in my head counters with *Was there ever a time when you weren't?*

"If things with him don't work out, give me a call. If they do, then I wish you two all the best."

I study David for a few moments, trying to take in every-thing he's said. "You're a good guy, David."

He gives me a smile and I give him a thank-you hug.

Then David gives Max a nod and walks out of the reception hall.

I don't quite know what to do. I haven't ever let myself think about what I would do in a situation like this. Actually, I haven't even had to stop myself from thinking about this scenario, because I've never imagined it. Yet the moment David says that I am in love with my best friend, I feel the truth of it burning in my heart. Like I've always known it was there, but haven't acknowledged it.

Plus, I don't know how Max feels about me. Sure, I know that he likes spending time with me and that we get along well. We wouldn't be best friends otherwise. But what about beyond that? He has definitely given me looks lately that I swear mean he sees me as more than a sister, but he hasn't acted any differently.

I've only been standing on the dance floor alone for a few seconds, as the band is playing a slower song, before Max says something to Bex's nieces and then crosses the floor in long strides to meet me. He puts his hands in his pockets before glancing at the door David just exited.

"He left?"

I nod.

"But he likes you."

I nod again but I didn't need to—there must've been an entire wordless conversation between David and Max as David gave him that nod because Max seems to understand what has happened.

"Are you okay?"

I meet his gaze and nod. My mind is a jumbled mess like it hasn't yet processed everything that has just happened.

But as I look into Max's hazel eyes, I feel like everything is okay. Max is here, and everything is good.

"Do you want to go sit down? Or do you want to dance?"

We are standing in the midst of a lot of couples dancing, and I realize that we are the only ones not moving. I don't know what I want yet—I just know that I want to keep Max close, so I put my wrists on his shoulders, my hands meeting at the back of his neck. His hands find my hips, and we dance to the slow music.

My mind is racing so much faster than my body is moving, though. It's as if years of romantic feelings toward Max have been in my brain, back in some hidden reserve I hadn't known about. And then David's parting words flung the gate wide open and everything is spilling out, flooding my mind with thoughts and feelings and possibilities. And images of the way Max has been looking at me. It's all more than I can take in.

And this music is way too slow for the speed at which my brain is moving. "Actually, do you mind if we go outside for some fresh air?"

"Not at all." He guides me through the crowd with his hand on the small of my back, and I soak in the touch. David's hand has been on my back a good portion of the time we'd been dancing, yet having Max's hand there feels so new. Like something I haven't experienced before. Like it's the first time feeling the sun shine on my face.

We walk through the door at the back of the reception hall and onto a balcony that runs the full length of the back of the venue, overlooking the lawns and gardens below, lights illuminating all the beauty in the darkness. The fresh air is cool, and as I breathe it in, it helps to calm my body.

My brain is still running too fast, though. I can't stand still, just looking out over the railing. I need to move. So I head toward the stairs leading down to the gardens. Max doesn't say anything—he just walks beside me like he's unsure what I'm feeling or what he should be doing right now.

I'm pretty unsure myself. All I know is that my feelings for him are so intense. How has this massive amount of feelings been trapped behind that gate? It seems impossible.

We walk, neither of us talking, until we reach a secluded alcove where the ground rises up on three sides. At the back, an impressive twelve-foot rock structure has water tumbling down it, like a waterfall. A koi pond is nearby, and the most beautiful flowers and greenery are all around, and everything is lit by lights at our feet.

Normally, I would love to just sit on the nearby bench and immerse myself in the peaceful surroundings until the moment they kick us out. Right now, though, I'm not feeling peaceful. I am full of questions that I need the answers to.

The main one is whether Max will ever see me as more than a friend. Or a sister.

I'm not sure what his answer will be. I face him, searching his eyes through the glow of the moon and the landscape lighting, trying to guess. Once before, I allowed thoughts of a romantic relationship with Max to invade my senses. Not to the extent of what has just been released in me now, but enough that I knew I wanted to pursue it. I waited weeks to act on it.

When I finally did, he pulled back just slightly enough to stop the kiss, but with an effort not to make me feel rejected. I still felt it, though. It hadn't been easy to switch back to just seeing him as a friend, but eventually, I did it.

Now, though, the thought of ever going back to just being friends seems impossible. What has been released at the opening of that gate now fills every space in my mind, expanding to fill every corner. And the longer it roams free, the more it's going to wreck me. I have to know how he feels now.

But I'm so scared. What if he still just thinks of me as a sister? If I can't trap these feelings back inside again, what will it do to me? To our friendship? What if he tells me he isn't interested? Can I handle that news? Or will it crush me?

It very well could. But I decide that not knowing is worse. I have to ask.

How, though? My mind keeps cycling through questions I could ask, but each sounds awful. Maybe instead of talking, I just need to act.

Heart pumping faster than a hummingbird's, hands shaking, breaths coming in small little puffs, I step closer to Max, searching his eyes. I don't find the answers there, but he also doesn't back away like he did a year ago. I move in closer, so we are only the smallest breath apart. He still doesn't pull away.

Feeling exposed and vulnerable and open to the worst pain imaginable, I make the decision to risk it all. I rise up on my toes and close the remaining distance, crushing my lips against Max's.

His arms immediately wrap around my back, pulling me

tight to him, that one motion wrapping a protective barrier around everything vulnerable, keeping me safe from harm.

I start the kiss as a desperate plea to know how he feels and he answers with the same desperate need. But then his kiss turns cautious and hesitant. Almost like he's just as afraid as I am of something happening that will break the magic spell we seem to be under.

Eventually, I pull away from the kiss just a couple of inches, but almost of their own accord, my arms around his shoulders still hold him tight like they're afraid that if I let go, he'll be gone forever. He keeps his arms just as tight around me.

"Max?" I whisper.

"Yeah?" he says, his voice low and gruff.

"Do you still think of me as a sister?"

He lets out a humorless chuckle enclosed in a single breath of an exhale. "No, Peyton. I never did."

# CHAPTER 14
## *Max*

I REPLAY Peyton's kiss next to the waterfall in my mind as I drive to Hidden Inn. Even though we've kissed quite a few times in the two weeks since that night, I still replay it several times a day. Every kiss with her feels significant, perfect, extraordinary. But none of them have the same raw, terrifying, exposed emotions that our first kiss had, where we laid everything on the line. Every kiss with her feels exactly right, and I wonder how I ever lived without them.

I pull into the long, curving driveway of the inn and park near the porch. I've made it up the stairs and almost to the front door when it flies open and Peyton steps out, her hands immediately finding my face, her lips pressing against mine. I put a hand on the small of her back and cradle her head with my other hand. Her lips move against mine, sending electricity flying in every direction.

When she pulls back, we stay close, smiling at each other,

her breath tickling my cheek. I move my hand slightly so my thumb can caress the skin of her cheek. "I missed you, too."

She smiles and drops her hand from my face, wrapping it in mine as we turn to walk into the inn. Can something this great possibly last?

This is my very first "Roommate plus significant others" dinner, and I've actually been slightly nervous, which I know doesn't make sense. I hang out with these same people all the time. Here. While eating food. I just never have at an official roommate dinner.

But it turns out it isn't that different from having pizza here—except there's better homemade food and everyone sits in the chairs the way they're meant to be sat in. It somehow feels like I belong. Like I've always been a part of this group.

Addison has made chicken piccata, which is apparently one of her specialties, and we mostly listen to stories about Bex and Roman's honeymoon in the Seychelles Islands, since they just got back yesterday.

"It's good to have you here, Max," Bex says as she reaches for a dinner roll from the middle of the table. "Are you in town for a while?"

I grin at Peyton. "It's good to be here. And, actually, I wanted to bring that up."

I hope Peyton will be interested in the plan I'm about to propose. I asked her once if she had much camping experience, and she said she'd wanted to go as a kid but that it wasn't in her dad's wheelhouse. Not wanting her to miss the chance entirely, I set up a tent in their backyard, made food on the barbeque, and we toasted marshmallows in the metal fire pit I bought. I so badly want her to experience real camping and see what she thinks of it.

"I'm heading into the mountains this weekend with three buddies from work that I camp with a lot, and I am hoping that you all might want to join us. We've got a big tent that everyone could fit in or smaller tents if you'd like to stay as couples, and as far as equipment goes, we have access to everything we could possibly need." I hold my breath as I wait for everyone's responses.

"I've always wanted to go," Peyton says. "Not that I have any clue how to camp."

Timini grins. "Neither do I, and I'm all for doing things I have no clue how to do. Count me in."

Addison and Bex both look at their husbands, a question on their faces.

"I can't," Ian says to Addison. "Roman and I are heading to Eugene Friday night to help my brother move, remember?"

Addison's face falls. "I forgot that was this Friday."

"And by the time we finish on Saturday and make the two-hour drive back, it might be after midnight before we get home. Depending on how much work there is to do, it might be Sunday morning. But you should still go if you want to. Camping here is pretty amazing."

Roman turns to me. "Your friends are experts, too, right?"

I nod. "A little too expert sometimes. Hunter knows practically everything there is to know about the outdoors. Emilio will make sure we have every gadget we could possibly need, and Leo—well, Leo keeps it real. And he whittles. They're all good guys. We'll keep everyone safe."

Roman looks at Bex, whose face clearly shows she's interested. "I think you should go, too."

Bex's eyebrows draw together. "Without you?"

He nods. "I think the four of you would have fun being in a tent together. A girls' trip, roughing it and braving the wild."

Bex looks at him for a long moment.

"Do you want to go?" Roman asks.

"I do. But I don't want you to miss out. Are you sure you don't mind me going when you can't?"

Roman nods. "I'll be here to see you off on Friday night, and then I'll be back by the time you're home on Sunday."

She turns back to me. "Can I film a *Bexlandia* episode while we are there?"

I'm so thrilled they want to come that I'd probably agree to anything. "Yes."

Peyton turns to her roommates. "We are going to go on an adventure!"

Seeing her get so excited about something so important to me is thrilling. I can't wait to show her firsthand all the things I love about camping, hiking, and spending time in nature. I so badly want her to love it. It feels like everything hinges on that.

Now I just need to plan the perfect trip so everything will go well and she will want to keep going with me forever. I'm a pro at this—it's practically in my job title. I'll have no problem at all making sure things go just right.

# CHAPTER 15
## *Peyton*

IT FEELS wrong to pack a suitcase for a camping trip, so I pack all the stuff I think I'll need into a big beach bag and a gym bag and heft them out onto the wrap-around porch.

Since Ian is driving his truck to Eugene and none of the rest of us drive vehicles meant to handle possibly rougher terrain, Bex swaps her car with her sister's Yukon. Bex's and Addison's husbands help to get everything loaded, then the guys head west on Highway 26 and my roommates and I head east. "It has been so long since I last went camping," Addison says. "I can't wait to get there!"

"And I can't wait to see what Max's other world is like." I pick up my phone and call him. When my call goes to Max's voicemail, I say, "It's five-thirteen, and we're just pulling out. See you at about six!"

Max went to our campsite a few hours ago because he wanted to get everything set up for us. There isn't cell service there, but there is a half mile down the road, so he asked me to leave him a message. He'll go check every half hour or so for a message from me so he'll know what time to expect us. How sweet is that? He really is the greatest guy.

I'm a little nervous about camping because I've never done it before. Not for real. But Max will help me through everything, and I'm glad that I'm going to experience something so important to him.

About a mile down the road from the inn, Bex slows and pulls the Yukon off to the side. "Look! They've started framing the walls!"

"Oh my stars," I say from the passenger seat, "you're going to have a real house soon." I let myself dream for a minute about what it might be like when I'm in Bex's shoes and have a husband and a house in the works. But lately, that feeling makes my guts get all tangled in knots.

It only takes about twenty-five minutes before we turn off the main road and head onto the tree-lined one leading into Mount Hood National Forest. Max camps all over Oregon and Washington and sometimes into California. I like that he chose a site so close to home for our first excursion.

"So," Timini says from where she and Addison share the backseat, "how are you and Max getting along now that you are dating?"

"Great! I mean, he's Max, so it's easy to get along great with him. That's why he's always been such a good friend."

The pause of voices in the SUV feels like a physical thing. A weight in the space.

"But?" Addison finally asks.

I look out the window at the mix of evergreens and

maple trees we pass by and take a deep breath. "I don't know. I guess I'm just worried." Then, I turn in my seat a bit so I can see all three of my roomies. "Okay, so that night at the wedding when David pointed out that Max and I were in love but weren't acknowledging it, there was so much swirling around in my head. Like a tornado hitting a cotton factory. But something changed for me that night.

"To find out that Max felt the same way about me was so exciting! The last couple of weeks have been a whirlwind of new things. And it's a different kind of new than I've ever experienced with other guys I've dated because it's Max. I mean, we've been friends forever. And now with the dating and the kissing and the cuddling up to him on the couch, it feels so incredible, you know?"

All three women sigh audibly.

"Turn right here?" Bex asks.

I look down at my paper with Max's instructions. "Zigzag, left, left, left, right. Yes." As Bex turns the vehicle onto the dirt road, I continue. "And in so many ways, it feels so right. Like things are finally the way they were always supposed to be.

"But I realized that even though so much changed for me that night at the wedding, nothing really changed for Max. Well, I mean, our whole relationship changed, but nothing changed *in* him if that makes sense. I don't know if it was just seeing him with your nieces, Bex, and thinking about how great of a dad he would be, or seeing the expressions that were crossing his face during your wedding ceremony that threw me off, or what.

"But, I've known him for four years, and he has always

said he'll never get married. He's convinced that most marriages are bad and almost none are good, and he's not willing to take the chance. Same with being a father. And he hasn't said that he feels any differently about it now."

"Have you talked to him about it?" Addison asks.

The SUV bumps around on the rock and dirt road that seems to have ruts going in every direction. I shake my head. "I think I'm afraid to hear the answer. He'll probably say he never wants to get married, and then what? I don't think I can just go back to the way things were—too much has changed between us. So will things just end? Am I supposed to go without Max for the rest of my life? I don't know if I can do that!"

I turn to look out the window again. "I am the worst at making important decisions. I need my mom." I've been aching for her lately as much as I did back when she first passed away. She probably would've helped me figure things out ahead of time so I wouldn't have found myself in this mess.

"What about—" Timini is cut off by a loud, deep popping sound, right before the Yukon tips to the right a bit.

Bex's attention flies from mirror to mirror. "Oh, no. What just happened?"

She brings the vehicle to a stop, and all four of us get out to see that the back passenger tire is completely flat.

"How?" Bex says. "The tread on these tires is way too thick for one of these rocks to pop it!"

Addison crouches down by the tire and sticks her head underneath to check out the backside. She emerges holding a little ancient screwdriver that's only about three or four inches long, including the handle. "This," she says, getting to her feet. "We must've run over it or something flipped it into the tire. It was stuck into the tire up to its handle."

I immediately try to call Max. "I don't have service. Do any of you?"

They pull out their phones, too, but nothing. I wasn't checking my phone during the drive, so I have no idea when we last had service.

"Don't worry," Bex says, heading around to the back of the vehicle. "One of my dad's requirements for me and my siblings to get a driver's license was to first show that we could change a flat tire. And I changed one on my car about a year ago, so I've got recent experience, too. We've got this, ladies. We just need to…"

She reaches the back of the vehicle as a collective, "Oh" sounds from all of us. All of our gear is blocking access to the tire.

It doesn't take long before all of our bags and bedding are in a pile on top of the dirt and rock road, the back of the Yukon is empty, and we're all looking for something on the floor of the vehicle to lift to get to the tire. I haven't exactly changed a flat tire before, but I'm pretty sure that's where they're kept.

"Where is it?" Bex says, baffled. Then, seeing a little hatch on the side panel, she opens it to check if the jack is inside. All it contains, though, is a stash of Bex's nieces' and nephews' stuffed animals.

Addison gets back down on the dirt road and looks under the vehicle. "It's mounted underneath."

I look over at all the stuff we already unloaded from the

back and try to think of something positive that came from it. More exercise?

Timini leans down to look. "Umm...how are we supposed to get it down?"

"Changing a tire is like baking a cake," I say. "We just have to follow the recipe." I go back to my seat and start looking through the glove box until I find the recipe—a.k.a. the owner's manual—and flip to the section about the spare tire. I walk back around to the back of the vehicle, shaking my head.

"Okay, so see that cup holder? The jack and tools are hiding under that."

Timini climbs into the back of the Yukon and pulls out the cup holder, then I point at the objects that are shown in a drawing in the owner's manual. "See those two spinny things? You unscrew one to get to some tools that look like rods and you unscrew the other to get to the jack.

"Then we connect the rods and stick them into a hole..." I look between the picture in the manual and the bumper. "Oh! It's behind that two-inch square on the bumper that just blends right in—we have to first pry it off or something —then we twist the rods to lower the tire. My stars, it's like they made it a scavenger hunt to see if people are smart enough to find everything."

Luckily for us, we're all smart. But that doesn't mean figuring it all out is easy. Also, jacks aren't designed to be put on super lumpy, bumpy, rocky, packed dirt roads. We know that now.

Another lesson learned: lug nuts are hard to loosen. And though it may sound like a good idea to put your entire weight on the big X-shaped tool to help get them not so tightly on, it's not actually wise to jump to land on the rod because when it does loosen, it might just send you flying off, landing you in a heap, half on the dirt road and half in the underbrush.

So now, I'm all hot and dirty, especially on my backside, and I've freed more than a few twigs from my hair.

I'm also really getting concerned about what has been keeping Max from coming to look for us. We should've arrived at camp about forty-five minutes ago, and we haven't even seen a single vehicle pass by.

It takes all four of us to heft the massive wheel off the SUV and then to get the holes in the rim of the spare tire lined up with the screw things sticking out. But we do it, and then take turns getting the lug nuts screwed onto the part sticking out through the wheel and tightened.

When we finally let the jack down, we all collapse against the side of the vehicle, exhausted, looking at the flat tire lying on the dirt road, hoping for some of our energy to return so we can get the heavy thing back underneath the vehicle and to get our gear loaded up again.

"I feel like I just wrestled a bear," Timini says. "And lost."

"This was way more difficult than changing the tire on my car," Bex says.

In a voice so weak it hardly sounds like Addison, she says, "We should take a victory photo."

I nod. "We should, because yay us." I was going to raise my arm in some kind of show of muscles or triumph but decide it's going to take all I've got just to pull out my phone.

Before I even open the camera app, I see the time. It's almost seven now and the sun is getting low in the sky. Surely Max knows by now that we've run into a problem. Why hasn't he come? Did something happen to him? Did something happen to all of them? Did bears attack the camp? Is he in trouble? Did he get his own flat tire? Does he need us to come to rescue him?

We really need to get going. I snap a picture of us all being exhausted first.

I've just pushed myself off the side of the SUV when I hear a vehicle's tires on the rocky dirt. My heart soars and excitement fills me at the hope of seeing Max and gives me enough energy to run a little way down the road to where I can look past the bend. Sure enough, Max is in the passenger's seat of his friend's truck. I let out the hugest breath of relief that he's okay and race to him as they come to a stop and he gets out.

He looks every bit as relieved to see me. He wraps his arms around me and pulls me in tight, then backs up, putting distance between us, looking me up and down. "Are you okay? I was so worried, especially when we couldn't find you."

"I'm fine. And you're fine?"

He nods and places a kiss on my forehead. Then he pulls another twig from my ponytail.

"Yeah," I say, "I took one for the team. I swear I'm a twig magnet. Which is okay—I'll take twigs over bugs any day."

"About time, slowpokes," Bex calls out.

Max's friend, Emilio, laughs. "You know, it'd be a lot

easier to find you if you stayed on the main road instead of turning onto some cabin's driveway."

I look up and down at the long road we're on. "This is a *driveway*?"

Bex groans. "Please tell me there isn't a cabin like twenty feet in that direction."

Emilio rises up on his toes. "I think I see one through the trees."

"Are you kidding or being real right now?" Timini asks. "Because if there is one, I'm just saying that they might have a hot tub and we deserve a good soak about now." Then she stands taller. "Or snacks. Did you bring snacks?"

"Even better," Emilio says. "We have dinner waiting back at camp."

Max chuckles but then turns all of his attention to me. He reaches a hand up and skims his fingertips down my cheek, along my jaw, and across my lips, all with an expression on his face like I'm adored and cherished and the most beautiful person he's ever seen. Even though I'm covered in dust, I'm sweaty, and there's probably more hair outside of my ponytail than in it at this point. I know that no matter what kind of pickle I manage to get myself into, he'll be there, helping or supporting me in any way that he can. He loves me that much.

Then he breathes, "I'm sorry we didn't find you sooner so we could've helped with all this." He pulls me in for a dusty hug before giving me the sweetest quick kiss and a squeeze of my hand and then heading to the Yukon.

He and Emilio get the popped tire mounted under the Yukon and heft our gear back inside the vehicle.

For our entire friendship, I've always noticed how good-looking Max is. But because we were just friends, I never let myself notice *too* much. Kind of like how you don't let yourself stare directly at the sun. So now that we're dating, watching him lift heavy things is different. It's suddenly okay for me to notice just how beautiful those shoulder and back and arm muscles are. I can't even believe it's okay for me to look now.

Once we're back in our vehicles, Max and Emilio lead the way to the camp, which ends up only being about an eight-minute drive. I can't believe we got so close before I led us off course. We pull to a stop first, and then Max directs Bex where to park the Yukon.

"Wow!" Addison says as she steps out. "I wish camping as a kid had been like this!"

I am speechless. The guys have set up two big tents at the far end of the camp. Right in the middle is a campfire surrounded by camp chairs, with a nearby picnic table and food tables. The entire area is enclosed by tall hemlocks and cedars and Douglas firs, their branches reaching out over the camp like they're protecting us, a ferny woodland at their base.

Mosses grow at the feet of the trees and up the sides and branches of the trees. And it smells incredible. Fresh and clean and earthy. It's as if we've stepped into another world that I hadn't fully known existed.

Emilio and Max's other friends, Hunter and Leo, go to work emptying all our gear from the SUV and transporting it to our tent. But Max grabs my hand and says, "Come on. I want to show you everything."

All four of us follow as Max points out our tent, how there's an extra tarp in case it rains, that there are restrooms down the road a ways, but that they've set up a portable latrine and shower, all of the gear they brought to make the trip more enjoyable, and which items he helped design. I look around, realizing all that he has done for me just so I can experience what he loves in as amazing a way as possible.

"And look," he says, "just over here we even have a stream! This is one of my favorite camp spots because it has everything."

The stream is only about twenty feet away from camp, the water in it looks cool and crisp, and the sounds it makes are musical and perfect. The way Max grins is so adorable that I just want to hold his face in my hands and admire it for ages.

# CHAPTER 16
## *Peyton*

I SNUGGLE down into my sleeping bag, trying to get warm now that we're no longer in front of the fire. Except for my dinner roll falling into the ashes from the fire (covering it in what Leo calls "nature's pepper"), dinner tasted amazing.

And except for a giant moth landing right on Max's face when he was giving me a goodnight kiss under the stars and causing me to scream before smacking him on the cheek to scare it off, it was the most amazing kiss ever.

And except for the fact that I left my pillow at home on the check-in desk of the lobby and am now using my gym bag stuffed with the clothes I was wearing earlier as a pillow, sleeping in a tent is a lot more comfortable than I thought it would be.

As Addison, Timini, and I are getting all situated, Bex comes in with a big mischievous grin and a bag of Chips Ahoy she found in the food bins. So we all sit up in our sleeping bags, eat cookies, and talk like we're at a sleepover.

We even film part of it for an episode on Bex's YouTube channel.

So after such a full day and such a late night, I have no problem drifting off to sleep to the sounds of the crickets and the gurgling stream.

———

My eyes fly open. What did I just hear? I have no idea what time it is, just that it's somewhere in the middle of the night.

There it is again. *Inside* the tent.

A crinkling sound. A scraping. Then nothing.

I'm sure I heard it this time. I hold my breath, straining to hear what it is. After a few moments of nothing, I figure it must be Bex shifting in her sleeping bag. I close my eyes and start to breathe normally.

Then the crinkling is louder, and I can tell it's not coming from Bex. I sit up, scrambling for my cell phone, and turn on the flashlight as quickly as I can.

A raccoon inside my tent freezes, his eyes shining in the light, his arm deep in the Chips Ahoy bag. And there's another raccoon just inside the tent opening. No, two! And three more just outside the tent door!

I scream. And not just any scream, but a horror movie bloodcurdling scream that could probably be heard three states away. I'm pretty sure the raccoons will be telling their grandkids about it someday. "Ah, yes cubs. We almost got away clean, but then she screamed, and we all knew just how badly we'd messed up."

Quick as a flash, all six raccoons scatter like a perfectly

executed heist gone wrong. I swear one does a backflip out of the tent and another disappears so quickly I'm convinced he teleported. The one with his hand in the bag, though, gives me a death glare before he skedaddles. Left in their wake is a mostly empty bag of cookies, three more people awake, and my racing, thumping, crashing heart.

About one second later, Max is at our tent door, barefoot, in sweatpants and a hoodie, his hair a mess, wielding a marshmallow roasting stick in his hands like a bat, and a wild and confused *I-was-sound-asleep-and-now-I'm-alarmed* look on his face. "What is it? What happened? Is there a bear?"

"Raccoons." I duck my head. "I didn't mean to wake everyone." Embarrassment at having screamed so loudly mixes in my chest with immense gratitude that Max would come to my rescue so quickly. And that marshmallow roasting stick? That thing means business, and he's gripping it like he'd actually be willing to take on a grizzly. Man, can he pull off *knight in shining armor* well, even when he's ripped from sleep in the middle of the night.

"But you're all okay?"

"Our heart rates are a little faster than they have a right to be in the middle of the night, but otherwise, we're right as rain." Which, I'm realizing, isn't a good metaphor now that I'm picturing how *not* right rain would be while camping. Of course, if Max was with me, anything would be right.

And now I'm wondering if I'm breathless because of the raccoons or because Max showed up in a hoodie, hair a mess, being all protective and heroic.

As he lowers the marshmallow stick, I can't help but think he's the most attractive human I have ever seen. How can he look so good at this hour? He should come with a warning label: May cause swooning and dizziness. I have to stop myself from fanning my face. My heart dances the salsa whenever I'm around him. How in the world am I ever going to live without him?

He says he's going to get something to help, disappears into the darkness for a moment, and then comes back holding a single twist tie from a bread bag. I half expected him to return with a dagger, or at least a bungee cord or something. Instead, I'm supposed to defeat the raccoon hordes with a teeny little twist tie?

He kneels down just inside our tent, then crawls to me and places the tie in my hand. "When I leave, pull the vertical and both side zippers together tight. Then put this through the little hole in all three zipper pulls and twist it. Then nothing will be able to unzip it from the outside."

He gives me the sweetest kiss, and then he backs out of the tent. Right before he zips it closed again, he grabs the cookie bag. "Oh, and keeping food away from your tent is a good idea, too."

"So… did the raccoons win?" Bex asks before collapsing back, making asleep breathing sounds before her head even hits her pillow. I have no doubt she'll have no memory of this in the morning.

Unlike me. I lie back down on my makeshift pillow, close my eyes, and try to calm my racing heart. But I can't help but replay over and over the moment when Max showed up instantly to defend my honor against raccoons. And how attractive he looked doing it. And how sweet he still was when he found out it was just raccoons in our tent and not a giant bear.

He's such a beautiful man. A beautiful man I know I can't have in my life for very long.

# CHAPTER 17
## *Max*

I WANT everything to go perfectly for Peyton's first camping trip. The guys have been completely on board with this plan, which is why they were willing to take off work three hours early to get camp set up. Yesterday didn't quite go as perfectly as I'd hoped, but with all I have planned today, it is sure to.

Well, okay, the morning hasn't been without its own issues. Leo slept the latest, like usual. When Emilio, our resident early-riser left the tent, he "accidentally" left it unzipped. The jury is still out on whether or not he lured an extended family of squirrels into the tent, knowing how much Leo fears anything with legs that isn't human, or if the squirrels sensed it on their own and thought terrorizing him might be fun.

Admittedly, seeing the horde of squirrels literally bouncing off the tent walls, all while Leo was in the middle of the chaos doing his squirrels-are-attacking dance, was kind of funny. But it probably didn't help me be convincing in my morning conversation with Peyton about how animals rarely get into tents.

"Need some help?" Peyton asks as she snuggles up next to me at the portable griddle where I'm making omelets.

I have spent so many hours daydreaming about moments exactly like this. Waking up to see her beautiful face. Having her snuggle up to me as I make breakfast. Sharing all of my life with Peyton.

Yet it all feels temporary, like this can't be real life, and real life is going to swoop in and change things before long. Unless I can make this weekend—or at least the rest of this weekend—perfect. If Peyton loves everything about being out in nature and wants to go with me on more camping trips, then maybe I wouldn't have to worry about losing who I am at my core.

"Nope. You always make food for everyone. This weekend is about you sitting back, relaxing, and enjoying nature while I make food for you."

She looks up at me with eyes that are so sweet and perfect that I could stare into them forever. I've enjoyed being friends with her over the past four years. During that time, I've daydreamed about a romantic relationship with her almost daily. Just imagining that has gotten me through some exceptionally tough days.

Actually living my daydreams has been beyond incredible. So much better than I ever imagined. Peyton is everything I want in a friend and everything I want in a partner. She makes me feel capable of reaching for my loftiest goals, desire to be the best man I can be, and so hopeful about everything. She sees the absolute best in me and helps me to see it in myself.

She gives me a quick peck on the cheek and joins the others standing around the campfire, trying to shake off the morning chill. That is good, too, because with her over there, I can admire how incredible she looks in jeans, a flannel shirt, hiking boots, and a ponytail.

Or maybe admiring her is a bad idea. I quickly flip the omelet I'm burning.

When I finish the last omelet, I join everyone else around the campfire and we all eat breakfast.

"You think I *lured* the squirrels into our tent?" Emilio asks, wearing a grin that doesn't do much to hide his guilt.

Leo shrugs. "I left the toy snake in your sleeping bag, so you're the most likely culprit."

Even if Leo doesn't see Emilio's guilt, it's obvious that Hunter does. But Hunter is smiling like stirring the pot is the game we're playing, so he says, "Not Max? You saw how easily he got them to follow him out of the tent."

"True," Leo says, dragging out the word as he turns on me. "You *did* seem to instantly know to cut up pieces of an apple to get their attention. And who else can lure squirrels with apple chunks in their hand? Only Snow White." Leo looks at the four women around the campfire. "This is why we are always trying to scare him or knock him into streams or lakes. The guy has nature on his side, so we have to do something to keep things even."

Then the three guys—my friends and camping buddies—go on to share a bunch of stories about me in the wilderness that I would've preferred not be shared. Maybe bringing them all along was a mistake after all. Especially because Bex is filming a lot of it, so it will likely make it into one of her episodes. There is so much laughing going on, though, especially from Peyton, that it can't be anything other than good.

Hunter tells a story from a few years ago about me being away from camp and looking for tinder for a fire. I had accidentally slipped a foot into an animal hole that had been buried by leaves and got a bit stuck. Then Hunter swears that a chipmunk came into camp and started chattering urgently like it was trying to tell them something. So they went out looking for me in the direction they'd seen me leave and rescued me.

The truth is, I hadn't even seen a chipmunk while I'd been searching for tinder. I don't tell them it was a coincidence, though, because no one seems to want to hear that part of the story. So instead, I just stand up and take a bow.

"All right. You've all had your morning coffee. I need to go get mine." I head over to the stream to free one of the cans of Mountain Dew that have been chilling with five of their friends in the cool water in the river. I've never liked the taste—or the smell, actually—of coffee. So even on the really chilly mornings in the mountains, I still go for my Mountain Dew.

I have to take a few steps onto rocks in the water to get to where the six-pack lies nestled. I'm almost to them when I hear some rustling in the bushes behind me. Of *course* they would come and try to get me to take a misstep and fall into the water. I call over my shoulder, "I know it's you, Leo, and Emilio. You're not going to get me that easily."

I do make sure I'm balanced a little more than normal,

just in case they jump out or throw something at me. Then I bend down and free one of the cans from the plastic ring that holds it to the others.

More rustling.

I turn around but don't see either of them. I know better than to let my guard down, though—they're both pretty good at hiding. So I step onto the rocks in the water carefully the rest of the way back to the shore, keeping my eyes toward the area with the rustling.

Then, to get the upper hand and keep them from knocking me off my game, as I leap onto the shore from the last rock, I scream, my arms raised high in the air, knowing it will make Leo yelp.

It's not Leo in the bushes, though.

It's a skunk.

I know the warning signs that skunks give before spraying—tail raised and shaking, stamping feet—but that's when the skunk sees you first and wants to warn you. We have both been so surprised by the appearance of each other that the skunk skips the formalities and goes straight to offensive mode. The animal shifts into a U-shape with both its face and hind end aimed toward me so quickly that I barely have time to turn, covering my face and head with my arms, before the animal sprays. And then we both run.

I hear the sounds of everyone reacting to the smell—and probably my scream that preceded it by about one second—before I even come around the edge of the bushes and trees to see them. And I get it. I'm barely keeping myself from gagging from the smell.

"Max, is that…you?" Emilio plugs his nose.

And that is the moment that everyone's faces go from scrunched at the bad smell to horrified. Especially Peyton's. I want to shout to the universe, *Didn't you know I needed this weekend to go perfectly?!*

"Did it get you in the face?" Hunter asks. When I shake my head, he says, "Good. Because that stuff's like pepper spray. Okay, we need to deal with this quickly."

Hunter is up, heading over to the supply bins.

"Tomato sauce!" Leo shouts, rushing to join Hunter at the bins. "I heard that helps."

Hunter shakes his head. "That's a myth. It just masks the scent for a bit. Skunk spray contains sulfur-based compounds called thiols. We have to break those down to get the scent to go away. The quicker the better."

"Should he go wash off in the river?" Addison asks.

"No. We need hydrogen peroxide, baking soda, and dish soap, and since Emilio is always prepared for everything, I'm sure we have some. Ahh," Hunter says, pulling the items from the bins and then grabbing the dishwashing tub. "Emilio, grab the shovel and go dig a shallow hole off in that little area surrounded by trees. We're going to have to use dish detergent, and we'll need to bury it. Leo, go grab a pair of Max's gym shorts from his bag. Does anyone have shampoo for greasy hair?"

"I've got some," Leo says from inside our tent.

Hunter throws a black garbage bag at me. "You go—" he waves his hand in the general direction he sent Emilio to dig the hole—"far away. Get your clothes in that bag and close it tightly, then put on the shorts."

When I planned our perfect camping trip, getting

sprayed by a skunk wasn't on the docket. Neither was having to strip down not far from where seven of my friends are, including the woman I've been dreaming about for years.

"You're totally going to have PTSD after this, aren't you?" Emilio asks as he finishes digging the hole I'll be standing in soon. "Post Traumatic Skunk Disorder. Hey, do you think this will affect your standing as Snow White?"

I give my friend a little shove, and Emilio laughs. "Hey, now. Don't get your stink too close to me."

A moment later, Leo sets down a jug of water and the shampoo, then tosses me my shorts, and I put them on. I have barely pulled them up when Hunter rounds the corner, lugging the dishwashing tub full of liquid, with Peyton beside him. Great. Couldn't she be far away and not be witnessing this scene?

Hunter sets down the tub and then stands. "I know this stuff works because I've used it before. And since we're doing it so quickly, I can pretty much guarantee it'll get rid of the smell completely." He hesitates for a moment. "You know if it was just us guys up here, I'd literally have your back, right?"

I nod.

"But, well, since Peyton is here and your back took the brunt of it, we thought it might be better if she was the one to wash it off."

Better? I know my face must be red because of how hot it is. *Better* would be Peyton not being within a hundred miles of this happening and no one who witnessed it ever speaking of it again.

Then Hunter gives a nod, like everything is decided, and leaves me standing in a hole and Peyton holding her fingers just under her nose in our little cove surrounded by trees and bushes.

"Okay," Peyton says, nudging the tub closer to me and bending down to get the washcloth from it. "We can do this. I've seen you shirtless before. I mean, not since we started dating, but this is no big deal."

The blush on her face says otherwise and kind of makes me just a bit more okay with her being here. And, okay, it may make me suck in my gut a bit.

She stands behind me and starts running the washcloth wet with Hunter's concoction over my back with one hand. I may be covered in stench and in a situation I hoped to never be in, yet I can't help but marvel at how amazing this feels, knowing the cloth is in Peyton's hand.

After a few times dipping it back into the solution, she starts washing with a little more pressure, reaching around me to put her other hand on my chest as a counter-pressure, and my heart rate and breathing kick up several notches. I close my eyes just to more fully take in the feel of it. Peyton makes a little *eep* sound that tells me having her hands on me is affecting her, too.

"Oh, my goodness. That little guy sure packed a punch, didn't he?" A moment later, probably when she realizes she has to take a breath, even if she doesn't want to, she says, "Wow. That was some impressive work. He deserves a medal. Maybe if he sees you're bringing him a medal and you turn on that fabled Snow White charm, he'll let you get close without retaliating."

I laugh along with her. No one can find something positive in a situation like Peyton can.

I'm all too keenly aware that she is rubbing her hands all over my back, shoulders, chest, and arms. Of course, if I'm going to have Peyton's hands all over my torso, I really would've chosen other circumstances. I know that when I look back at this skunky situation, what I'm going to remember is this moment, with Peyton's hand on my chest while she washes my backside. I'm hoping that the memory that sticks with Peyton is similar and that she doesn't just take away from this a strong association between me and this stench. I'm hoping that part doesn't stick with her for long at all.

I'll give her something better to associate with me tomorrow morning. Before we break camp, we are going to head to French's Dome to do some rock climbing and rappelling. I know that for most people, watching a climber is impressive. I really hope she'll think so, too, so I can earn back whatever masculine points I've lost by my unfortunate skunk encounter.

"Okay, I think the back and your sides are done. Do you want me..." She motions at my chest. "Or would you rather..."

She has rested her hand on my chest plenty of times over the past few weeks—I remember each time rather vividly. She has laid her head there, too. In fact, she has fallen asleep during movies leaning against my chest plenty of times before that. It's different here, though, with me facing her as I stand bare-chested in the woods, covered in skunk.

If I wasn't worried I might get some of the thiols, or

whatever Hunter called the stink molecules, on Peyton, I would pull her in close and drop her into a dip or something, just to ease the awkwardness.

"How about I wash my chest and legs and shampoo my hair, and then you rinse me and give me a good smell test to make sure we got it all." Skunks aim for the eyes. Since I turned quickly enough and ducked my head, my back and arms have taken most of it, anyway.

Once I get myself washed and Peyton rinses me, I try to not let my pecs, biceps, or any other muscles twitch or involuntarily flex as she gets super close and smells my back, chest, and arms. I am successful a good seventy percent of the time. Those last two twitches were beyond my control.

And then she smiles, smacks me on the rear, pronounces me skunk-free, and walks back to join the others in camp.

As I watch this woman I've been in love with for so long walk back, her flannel shirt wet and pushed up to her elbows, water splotches all over her jeans, a few small locks of hair falling out of her ponytail, I can't help but smile, too.

# CHAPTER 18

## *Peyton*

AS WE GET to the end of the short walk between the parking lot at the trailhead and French's Dome, the tall canopy of evergreen trees opens up to show a massive hunk of rock that shoots up from the ground like someone planted a little rock seed, watered it, and then a few hundred years later, it grew to the size of a skyscraper.

"You're going to climb that thing?" I ask Max. I probably shouldn't let my voice tremble at all—I don't want to psych him out. But man, that is tall. And straight up. And pretty impossible-looking.

Max doesn't look psyched out, though. He looks more than a little confident.

"Wait, you've climbed this one before?"

"This will be time number five."

I just look up at the massive structure in awe. "How did this thing even get here?" It's not part of a mountain. It's simply here, acting like it's not strange to be right in the middle of the Oregon forest.

As I tear my eyes from it to look at Max, he says, "It's a volcanic neck core. Whatever else used to be around this eroded away over who knows how long, leaving this beauty as a gift to climbers."

I've heard Max talk about climbing plenty of times, and I've always pictured it like an indoor climbing wall, except outdoors. The scale of it is so far beyond anything I've imagined.

As all four of the guys get their harnesses on, check all their gear, and inspect the rope for any damage, I take plenty of pictures. And when it gets to be Max's turn to climb up, I take about a billion more. The man just looks so incredible as he makes his way up the side of the rock. As each arm reaches up, his hand searching for a handhold, I watch those arm and shoulder and back muscles and can't help but think about yesterday when I was washing them.

"I think I'd be passing out at that spot right there," Addison says. "How can they convince themselves to climb so high?"

"That's just straight-up impressive," Bex says, aiming her video camera at them. "It looks fun, but I don't know if I could do it."

"Me neither," I say. "I've always wished I could be as brave as Max. I swear he can accomplish anything, no matter how impossible it seems. He just always finds a way."

Timini chuckles. "Girl, you are so gone for this boy."

I really am. But how could I not be? He is just so inspiring! So comfortable and confident. Daring and adventurous.

I grew up having so many things done for me that when I decided I was going to be independent, not get any financial help from my dad, and start my own business, a lot of things were really hard. And there were so many times when I wasn't sure if I could even do it. But Max was so good at encouraging me when I wanted to give up and inspiring me to find ways of doing things that I hadn't ever thought of.

He feels like peace and acceptance and home. And how can a girl not be gone for that?

Somewhere around the halfway-up mark, though, my feelings switch from admiring everything about him that brought him to the point where he can accomplish a feat like this, to fear.

He's just so high up! I know he has a rope connected to his harness, and that the rope is going through some kind of bolts in the rock itself. But it just looks so dangerous.

I've known that he does things all the time like paragliding, cliff-jumping, mountain biking over rough, steep terrain, and sleeping in places where bears could probably wander, but I haven't imagined any of it being as dangerous as how things appear right now. He looks so teeny being so high up, and he still has so far to go! What if his arms get tired before he gets to the top and he just can't keep going?

And before I know it, the injuries he had when he showed up to his mom's house while I was cooking dinner —from falling down the mountainside on their hike—come to mind. And all the others I've seen over the years. Sore muscles. Stitches. A broken finger. Bruises all over. So many bruises.

Now that I'm seeing how scary his adventures are in

person, I suddenly wonder if I can handle knowing how badly he could get hurt every time he goes on a trip. As I hold my breath when he gets to a really difficult spot where he can't seem to find a foothold, I'm not sure.

# CHAPTER 19
## *Max*

IF ONE OF the guys is holding a stopwatch, I'm sure I've just gotten a record time climbing French's Dome. This might be my fifth time climbing the monolith-like rock formation hidden in the evergreens, but it's the first time I've pushed myself so hard. If it was just the guys with me, I would've paused more on my way up, letting my legs hold my weight for a few moments whenever they were on steady footholds.

But this time, Peyton is watching and taking pictures, and I really want to impress her. So even though my legs and arms burn and my fingers ache from holding on to the tiniest handholds, I push on.

This is one of my favorite places to climb, and it attracts crowds of climbers. The rock is practically straight up and, at one hundred twenty feet tall on the part I'm climbing, it's an impressive height without being massive. And it's full of hand and footholds that are marked with chalk by plenty of other enthusiasts who have climbed the route before us. Two or three climbers are making their way up each route around the dome right now, and people are even waiting below for a turn.

Leo crests the top first, hooking the lead rope into the bolts in the rock. Emilio goes up next, and he offers me a hand once he gets to the top. As Hunter makes his way up the rock face last, I, along with half a dozen other climbers who also stand at the top, look out at the view. For as hidden as this place is from the roads around it, this vantage point allows me to see everything—Mount Hood, the mountains beside it, the wilderness surrounding it—and it seeps into my soul. Scenes like this are my fuel. My stress-reliever. The thing that keeps me going.

I offer a hand to Hunter as he gets to the top, and the four of us stand, side by side, looking out over the edge at Peyton and her roommates, who are waving, whooping, and taking pictures. My chest swells with pride.

Then Hunter's phone dings with a text, and all of our attention goes to him. There wasn't reception down below—I hadn't imagined there would be up here. Hunter pulls his phone from a side pocket on his climbing pants and looks at the screen, brows drawing together, before he looks at us, alarm and worry all over his face.

"Tami's having a miscarriage. She's been trying to get hold of me—she's at the hospital now. I've got to go."

Hunter immediately goes to the edge and picks up the rope, but I put a hand on his shoulder. "We've all got to get down before we can leave. Let your body rest for a minute and let your heart rate calm down so you don't make a fatal rappelling mistake. Let Leo and Emilio go first."

Hunter nods, and I stand next to my friend, my arm around his shoulder, as Emilio connects his harness to the lead rope and makes his way down while Hunter texts his wife to let her know he'll be there soon.

"I shouldn't be here," Hunter says. "What was I thinking? I should've been home with her. Or I should have been somewhere with cell reception. What if she's not okay? She shouldn't have to face this alone."

Over and over, Hunter's worries travel in circles, coming back around to the same thing—that being out here, pursuing our passion, kept him from being a good husband. I try to calm my friend so he'll be going into the descent with as clear a head as possible. But the truth is, all of Hunter's fears and concerns mirror my own fears and concerns.

Once both Leo and Emilio are on the ground, I help check Hunter's gear, making sure he has redundancies and that everything is safe and good to go before rappelling down. I know that most accidents happen during the descent and how important it is to have your head in the game, so I find myself holding my breath nearly the entire time that Hunter is climbing down. Once he finally steps foot on the ground, I let out a massive breath of relief.

Peyton blows me a kiss from one hundred twenty feet below, so I pretend to catch it and put it in my pocket. Then I hook up my own gear, making sure everything is hooked through both loops in my harness, that the lead rope is connected correctly in the chain in the rock, and that I have redundancies and everything is safe, too. My own head is full of too many worries, and I'm not about to make a mistake.

As I rappel down, my feet landing against the same stones I used as hand and footholds on the way up, I force my focus to stay on tending the friction hitch with one hand and feeding the rope through with the other.

It mostly works, until thoughts and worries about whether I'm going to be able to be everything Peyton deserves keep creeping in. *Focus. Focus on the rope.*

About halfway down, things are going well, and I've fallen into the familiar rhythm, letting the joy of the height and my surroundings push everything else out. Then, a climber who is ascending with a lead rope to my left and a good eight feet higher up the dome loses his grip and falls. He's almost to the next bolt, which means that he's falling the biggest distance possible—probably ten feet.

It's nothing. It happens all the time. Except this climber somehow gets his foot stuck in the crevice he planted it in, throwing him upside down as he falls. As the man swings wildly, trying to right himself, he bounces against the rock and swings back, heading straight toward me.

All of my training tells me that if something is ever coming at me from above or from the side, I should cling to the rock face and keep myself as flat against it as possible. If my head was in the game instead of on the beautiful woman watching from below and how to keep her in my life, I know I would've done just that. Instead, I let my normal, human reactions through. The one that says to reach out and try to catch the person coming at me, to cushion them.

The force of the climber plowing into me is enough to

knock the breath out of me a micro-second before my shoulder is wrenched back and smacks against the rock. I nearly lose my grip on the rope and fall a few feet before instinct makes me grab tight with my uninjured arm. I swing wildly back and forth, the pain in my shoulder so sharp and unrelenting I have trouble thinking of anything other than it.

Eventually, with sharp intakes of breath sucked through my clenched teeth, I start to hear the shouts of the people below. Not enough to tell what they're saying, but enough to know they're there. With one good arm and the small amount I manage to force my injured arm to do, I continue my descent, much more jerkily than the first half.

By the time my feet touch solid ground, I collapse from the pain, a swirl of activity around me, a bevy of questions I can't make out or answer.

Once using my arm is no longer a life-or-death necessity, the mind-numbing pain slowly lessens just enough that it's not the only thing I can focus on. I manage to get to my feet and into Hunter's truck with Hunter's and Peyton's help. Then the three of us head to the hospital while the others go back to pack up camp.

Every bump in the road jerks my arm enough to send a new wave of sharp pain, but Peyton is here, trying to hold me so the bumps are lessened. With her at my side, I can handle this just fine. Her presence tempers the pain and clears my mind.

# CHAPTER 20

## *Peyton*

WATCHING the doctor put Max's shoulder back into its socket is the most painful thing I've ever witnessed. And that's just for me! I can't imagine how bad it is for Max. Thankfully, they give him something for the pain before they set it. I'm not sure it has actually started working yet, though, based on how much pain Max seems to be in while they do it.

I just keep reliving that moment in my mind when the other climber fell and smacked into Max. The way that I can tell, even from sixty feet below, that his shoulder bent unnaturally. The way his body bounced back after hitting the rocks so forcefully. That bit of a drop that seized my heart and made me worry he was about to fall all the way. I hope the horror of it isn't still showing on my face. I'm trying to be strong for Max.

"Okay, we got it set," the doctor says. "My guess is that you won't need surgery, but we're going to send you in for an MRI to see what damage was done. You'll need to follow up with an orthopedic surgeon in the next couple of days, and you'll need their clearance before climbing again.

"And don't drive with that pain medicine we've got you on. But we'll get you into a sling before you go. Keep it on— it'll help you heal and remind you not to use it." The man gives him a sympathetic smile. "It was a bad one. You're going to be feeling it for a while. Be careful with it."

Then the doctor turns and gives me a sympathetic smile, too. Like he can tell that Max is an adventurer and it's going to be hard to get him to not use his arm, and there won't be much I can do about it.

Once everyone else is out of the room and we're just waiting for someone to come take Max to the MRI machine, I sit on the side of his bed, careful not to bump him, and hold his hand. "I'm sorry you got so injured."

He lifts my hand and brushes his lips across my knuckles. "I'm sorry the camping trip was such a bust."

"What are you talking about? I got great food, prepared and handed to me by the most gorgeous server ever. And I got to hang out in the most amazing scenery and fall asleep to the sound of crickets. And I got to witness Leo freak out more about acrobatic squirrels than I did about thieving raccoons, which was pretty satisfying. Actually, I think he would freak out about spiders more than me, too, which is saying something."

Max gives a weak but amused smile. "I've seen you both happen upon a spider, and I can confirm that he freaks out more."

"See? And that's good to know. I like not being the one

with the most extreme reactions. Plus, I got to wash skunk off you, and that was pretty great." I can feel the blush on my cheeks. That part had been pretty great. Even if I had to turn away from him every few moments to get a breath of fresh air.

It makes me smile that he blushes a bit, too.

My phone lights up with a text—Timini is asking for an update. So I quickly type that Max had a dislocated shoulder and that we should be leaving in the next hour or so.

> Timini: Oh, I'm so glad it wasn't worse!

> Timini: We got camp all packed up, and Addison and I are here at the hospital—we brought your car. They wouldn't let us come and give you the keys (probably because we smell like campfire and are covered in dirt from head to toe), but they are with the check-in nurse. We'll be home making food.

When they take Max to get an MRI, I call my dad.

"Hi, Daddy!"

"Hi, Sugar Bug."

"Do you mind if I cancel coming over for dinner tonight? I'm in the hospital with Max."

"Oh no!"

"He dislocated his shoulder while he was mountain climbing. He'll be okay, but I think I should help take care of him tonight. Is that alright with you?"

"Of course it is."

"Daddy, are you okay?"

"I'm fine."

I'm not sure I believe him. "You're sounding…off."

"I'm fine. Really. You take care of Max—don't worry about me."

I glance at the hallway they took Max down. I really hope he'll be okay soon. It doesn't look like the kind of injury he'll recover from as quickly as he usually does. "Are you sure?"

"Very. Want to reschedule for tomorrow?"

I tell him yes, we work out a time, and then hang up. And I immediately go back to worrying about Max.

---

It takes a lot longer than I think it will to leave the hospital and get Max to his apartment. I get him settled in his bed with the big fluffy couch pillow from the living room that I gave him last Christmas propping him up, his regular pillow just under his elbow helping to support the weight of his arm. I get him water, his laptop so he can watch a show, and am about to make him some soup when I get a call from a local number and answer it.

"Is this Peyton Abernathy?"

"It is."

"This is Sue from Kaiser Sunnyside Medical Center."

*Kaiser Sunnyside?* That's not the hospital I was just at with Max. I look over at him, dread already filling me.

"Your dad wanted me to let you know that an ambulance just brought him in for a possible heart attack. The doctors are checking him out right now."

Fear clutches at my heart just like it had weeks ago when he had his first one. "I'll be right there."

As soon as I hang up the phone, I stand, frozen, my mind and heart racing, my body not knowing which direction to go.

"Peyton," Max says, reaching his good arm out toward me. "What happened?"

"My dad. They think he might've had another heart attack."

Max's eyes grow wide. "Go. I'm fine."

"Max, you're not! Your shoulder wasn't even connected to your body a couple of hours ago. You have bruises everywhere, you're on pain medicine, and you nearly died!" My breathing is so fast I worry I'll pass out, but my heart is so afraid for the two men I love most in the world.

I let Max pull me to sitting on the edge of his bed, and he runs a hand down my arm. "Shh. Breathe with me."

I match my breathing to his. Slow and steady. In and out. It doesn't take long before my nerves don't feel quite so much like a train that has left the tracks and is barreling down a mountainside.

"Look at my eyes."

I do, and those green eyes capture me, holding me up, keeping me strong.

"I am okay," he says, stressing each word. "You have me set up like royalty in here. I'm banged up all over, sure, but my legs still work. I've been injured pretty bad before and have been just fine. I will be this time, too. Go to your dad, stay calm while you're driving, and keep me updated."

I stand but give him one last long gaze before my legs

pull me away and to the front door. He is strong. He is always so strong.

———

My dad looks so weak as he lies in the hospital bed in the thin gown, wires coming out from the neck and arm openings, all hooked to beeping machines that surround him like a silent army protecting their king.

"Hey, Sugar Bug. I didn't mean to alarm you."

A nurse is on one side of the bed, checking something with the machines, and the doctor is on the other side, looking tall and in charge in her white coat. So I stand at the bottom of the bed, wishing I could just hurry to my dad's side and wrap my arms around him.

The doctor reaches her arm out toward me, her dark skin such a contrast against her coat. "You must be Peyton," she says as she shakes my hand. "I'm Doctor Lewis. Your dad gave us a bit of a scare. But we've had the heart monitors hooked up to him for a good forty-five minutes now, and things are looking good. It doesn't appear to be a second heart attack."

"It doesn't?" Relief whooshes out of me.

"A lot of things can feel like a heart attack, especially in the first few months after a major one, like your dad had before. Even indigestion can feel like it's a legitimate problem. I'm glad he came in."

"The doc told me I was being a wimp." My dad may look weak, but that doesn't stop the teasing glint in his eye. It makes me happy to see it.

"No." The doctor shakes her head and chuckles. "I told him it's sometimes hard to tell, and it's a lot better to be overly cautious than under. We still aren't ready to give him a clean bill of health, either. We'd like to keep him overnight for observation."

Once the doctor and the nurse leave, I give my dad that hug. But it's a slow, careful hug that doesn't bump any of those wires. Then I pull a chair up close to his bedside and hold his hand.

"I'm sorry to make you go from one hospital to the next, Sugar Bug. I should've waited until they decided what was going on with me before calling you."

"No, it was good to call me at the beginning. Or to have told me you were worried when I called earlier."

He shrugs. "I was still convincing myself it was nothing when I talked to you. Plus, you've had quite the day, I'm sure."

I feel like I've run two back-to-back emotional marathons today. I can't believe it was just this morning that I woke up from my second night in a row of actual camping in the actual forest, and my second time waking up to Max making me breakfast.

Since then, I have experienced two separate moments where I feared for the lives of the two men most important to me and have sat in two different hospital rooms, holding each of their hands. And twice, I have felt torn about where I should be.

When I called my dad, I already knew that Max likely wasn't going to need surgery and that he would be going home soon. It felt like an easy choice to make at the time to stay with him instead of going to my dad's for dinner. But I'd felt in my gut that something was wrong with my dad, and I chose to ignore it. I should've recognized that it was something more serious. I should've chosen to go be with him. What if he hadn't called 911 quickly enough? What if he had really needed me there and I wasn't?

Sure, today worked out fine. But what if it hadn't? I glance at the screens of all the machines just to assure myself that he is actually, really okay.

"I wish Mom was here."

My dad squeezes my hand. "I miss her too."

"I need her to make my decisions for me." I need it desperately.

"What kind of decisions?"

Well, all of my decisions today, for one. And all of my dating decisions. Whether I should've started dating Max. All of my Max decisions, actually. Whether or not I should have bought those uncomfortable but super adorable heels last week. But mostly everything to do with Max. I wave my hand around, trying to encompass everything. "All of them."

He chuckles softly. "You know your mom wouldn't have made them for you."

"Yeah, she would have. She always did. I trusted her to make the right choice for me so much more than I trusted myself." No, that should be present tense. It's not like I trust myself any more now than I did as a kid.

My dad shakes his head. "Even when you were a little girl, you struggled to take risks, regardless of how badly you wanted the payoff. On the playground, if you brought your little plastic dump truck and you saw a group of kids playing with their trucks in the wood chips, you'd be afraid they might not want you to join and so you'd sit and play by yourself. If you saw a puddle that you weren't sure you could jump all the way over, you'd take the really long way around to avoid it.

"Your mom never told you to go play with the kids or try to make the jump. Your mom was just really good at seeing what your passions were. Or really good about getting you to talk about them. Then she would give you a boost of encouragement to take the risks. She never made the decisions. That was all you."

Yes, my mom saw my passions and was great at getting me to talk about them. But she also told me if pursuing something was a good idea or not. So if my passion was to run across the street to smell a pretty flower and a car was coming, my mom helped me make the right decision then, too. It's my dad who gives me boosts of courage to take risks but doesn't make decisions for me.

And right now, I really need someone by my side to tell me when I'm running out into traffic where Max is concerned.

# CHAPTER 21
## *Max*

THERE IS nothing like the call of nature to remind me that, although my shoulder took the brunt of that hit, the entire left side of my body smacked into the uneven rock. And to let me know exactly how difficult everything is with one arm in a sling. Or how much the tiniest jostling makes everything hurt.

After washing one hand without the aid of the other, I head back into my room and take one long look at my bed. I don't want to be here. I just need to get better already. Being this injured is ridiculous.

I have thought through my rappelling accident several times, each time trying to figure out what I should've done differently, but the nature of a freak accident is that you can't really plan for it. Yes, I could've hugged the wall, like I'd been taught, but the other climber and I still would've collided, and I still would've taken the worst of it. And since, as a climber, you can't plan for freak accidents, you just have to expect that you'll get blindsided by one at some point.

But did it have to happen during my camping trip with Peyton?

Instead of getting back into bed, I shuffle into my living room and look long and hard at the couch. I know that moving from standing to sitting will hurt, so instead, I choose to just flop down on it. Okay, so that might not have been the best choice.

I had so badly wanted everything to go well at the campout. I wanted Peyton to love the experience. I wanted to know that if we can handle a camping trip together—something that one of us loves and one of us is inexperienced at—then we can handle any experience either of us has. A trip gone well would also confirm that I can, in fact, do what I love most and get married to the person I love most. I know how important marriage and family are to Peyton, and I will never ask her to give those up just so she can be with me.

But instead, more things went wrong on the trip than I've ever had go wrong in one single trip before.

Which reminds me that I don't actually know where my bag of skunk-scented clothes currently is.

Not only was the trip a disaster, but it made Peyton not be with her dad when he needed her. Because if we hadn't been on that trip, I wouldn't have gotten injured, and she'd have gone to his house for dinner. And now, because I'm on some stupid medication, I can't even drive to join her at the hospital and support her while she's waiting for news about her dad.

How can I make sure things between us work out if I can't get one weekend to work out?

I think about Peyton being at her dad's side at the hospital and about how she grew up with the perfect example of a marriage right in her own home. Then I glance at the scrapbook that my mom gave me. It still lies, unopened, on my coffee table, and I have no intention of opening it anytime soon. I don't need the reminder that my genes come from a couple of people who couldn't stand to be married and made absolutely terrible spouses.

And that I might never be able to be everything Peyton needs me to be.

# CHAPTER 22

## Peyton

AS I WALK through the hospital hallways, I try to convince myself that it's better to drag my tired body out to my car and not lie on the floor right here and just stay unconscious for about two years in an attempt to recover from today. My dad is finally sleeping and I want to do the same, but I am too worried about Max for sleep.

So, even though it is nearing eleven, I gather all my extra energy reserves and drive to his apartment instead of driving to Quicksand. Well, I do after I find a soup and sand- wiches shop that is still open and get him some chicken noodle soup. It is as close to homemade as I can get, and I am convinced that it helps heal a body, not just a cold.

When I pull into Max's apartment's parking lot, I text to see if he is still awake. If he isn't, I plan to use my key to leave the soup and check on him to make sure he is okay. Because if I don't, I won't be able to sleep no matter how tired I am.

He texts back that he is, so I order him not to get up and tell him I will unlock the door myself. I am surprised to find him on his couch instead of in his bedroom.

"Max!" I set down my things and rush over to him. He looks so much worse than when I left. I shouldn't have stayed at the hospital with my dad for so long. "Are you okay? What's wrong?"

He shrugs with his good shoulder like he doesn't have the energy to do anything more. "I didn't know you'd be back tonight. How's your dad?"

"They don't think it was a heart attack. He's okay, but they are keeping him overnight. Let me help you get into bed. You must be so tired. Oh! Food! It's probably been way too many hours since you had anything to eat." I turn and grab the container of soup I set on the coffee table and hand it to him. "Your body needs fuel to heal. Let me get you a spoon."

When I come back from the kitchen and hand it to him, he says, "You don't need to take care of me."

I scoff. "Obviously I do. Look at how much worse you've been doing without me here."

He gives me a sad smile. There is more to it than sadness at getting injured, though. I study him for a long moment, trying to figure it out. Finally, he puts the spoon and soup down on the coffee table, the lid still on it. "I'm not good enough for you."

"That's the pain medicine talking. You know you're perfect."

"It's not the pain medicine talking."

"Oh no—did it wear off? I haven't paid attention to the

time." I grab the medicine bottle to see how often he should take it.

"Peyton."

He grabs hold of my hand and gives it a tug, so I sit down on the couch next to him.

"I can't get married. I can't be a dad."

I stare at him, confused. The words coming out of his mouth don't seem to be related to anything going on, so I wonder what has been beating around inside his head while I've been gone. "Max, you'll be fine. Before you know it, you'll be back to doing the same things you used to do. This injury isn't going to stop you. Just wait for your follow-up appointment with the orthopedic surgeon. He'll look at the MRI and make a game plan, and everything will be okay."

"Everything won't be okay. Not with us."

"Oh." I feel like my heart is collapsing down into itself at the words, trying to protect itself from what is coming.

"You deserve the perfect husband. Kids. The perfect family, the white picket fence, all of it. I really want you to have all of it. But I can't give it to you."

No, no, no. I cannot be getting the "You're the perfect girl...for someone else" speech. Especially not from Max. I stand and pace back and forth in the three feet beside his coffee table, trying to get my heart to stop racing like it is determined to take home the gold. "You're injured. This is just because of that accident. We should talk about this later."

"This isn't because of the accident."

"Are you saying we should stop dating? Because I don't know how to do that, Max!" I've been worrying about this moment coming ever since I made the foolish decision to kiss him at Bex and Roman's wedding. But I am so very tired, and the words I am hearing don't feel real. Like they are happening in a dream and I am watching from afar.

"I don't, either. But we are going to have to figure it out."

His face is full of so much pain. It is etched in every line, in the curve of his mouth, the shape of his eyes. I want to hug him and hold him and lay my head on his strong chest and tell him everything is okay and make all the pain go away. I step closer and reach an arm toward him. "Let me help you get into bed."

"I don't need help."

His words feel like a slap, and my eyes fall to my arm that is still stretched toward him before I drop it to my side.

"Peyton—"

I meet his eyes.

"I'm sorry."

———

I drive away from Max's apartment, too mentally exhausted to process what has just happened. My eyes are blurry from tears, my breath is hitching, and the inn is too far away to drive to in my current state. So I choose the closer option and drive to my childhood home.

Even though I've known that Max never wants to get married, I haven't realized how much of me has been holding out hope that I'm going to be the one to make him feel differently. I've seen the pain in his eyes. We've been such good friends for so long that I know it couldn't have been easy for him to end things. I don't question how much he cares for me—we wouldn't have been such good friends for so long if he didn't. So it's stupid to feel like I haven't been enough for him when I went into it knowing that he doesn't want to get married.

Yet I feel that way anyway.

With my dad in the hospital, the house feels empty and alone. Fitting. The darkness is pressing down on me, though, so I flip on every light as I make my way from the front door to my old bathroom to take a shower. Then I put on some fluffy Hello Kitty pajamas that I haven't worn since probably my sophomore year of college and thank my lucky stars that my dad has left my bedroom the same as the day I moved out. With the bedroom light still on, I crawl into my old bed that I haven't slept in for years and stare at the wall covered in business cards.

I stared at this same wall for hours as a kid and a teen, letting the power of so many fulfilled dreams fuel me. Inspire me. Make me feel like anything is possible. Now I look at them and wonder something I haven't ever wondered before. All of the people on the business cards obviously had a dream that they brought to life. Did any of them then have to walk away from it?

If so, how did they survive it?

I started off my week of fifteen dates hoping to find a date for the wedding and a future husband, and not only ended with neither, but ended minus one best friend. One best friend who, for a glorious moment, was also my boyfriend.

I need my mom.

# CHAPTER 23
## *Max*

MY MIND IS A TUMULTUOUS MESS. The kind of mess best fixed by a hike up a mountainside or a good long jog. But with the way my body feels, both are out of the question, so I instead take a slow, careful walk along the Quicksand River trail.

Like I have since the moment last night when I basically told Peyton that I don't want any of the things that she wants, I've been replaying that conversation in my head. What was I thinking?

Okay, I know exactly what I was thinking—that I'm afraid. Scared to death, more like. Why do I have no fear when it comes to jumping off a cliff into the water down below, soaring through the air on a paraglider, climbing a sheer face with nothing but a bolt and a rope keeping me from falling, or eating food that Leo cooks over a campfire, but I run away screaming from a life spent with the woman I love?

Why does the big M-word cause me to quake in my well-designed hiking boots? I love Peyton. I love being with her. The thought of *not* having her in my life is actually even more terrifying than marriage. So why did I tell her I wanted to stop dating her?

It hasn't even been a full day, and already I have to stop myself from texting her out of habit. I want to find out how her dad is doing. Give her an update on how I am feeling this morning. I want to text her a picture of how the sun is glinting off the river as it goes over two boulders in one area. I want to ask how she slept last night. When I can see her next. What she has on the docket for today. I want to see her smile, hear her voice, wrap my arms around her, and tell her I love her.

Instead, I am hiking alone, doing none of that, and wondering how I can make it through today without her, let alone a lifetime. In one single fear-filled night, I lost the love of my life and my best friend all at once.

# CHAPTER 24

## *Peyton*

AFTER THE WEEKEND I've had, it would be as good as finding a twenty-dollar bill in a jacket I haven't worn for months if I had a day with no clients so I could recover. Instead, I drag myself, puffy-eyed and exhausted, to my first client's at eight a.m. sharp to make a week's worth of meals for a family who is usually three but who currently has a married son with a wife and two kids staying with them for the week, so it became a family of seven.

Then I go straight to another client's home who always insists I cook at her house, even though her kitchen is the size of a child's play set. Then I stop and check on my dad, who is back home again and doing great. His nurse is staying until he goes to bed, which makes me feel a ton better, even if it agitates him. Then I shop for the groceries I need for the first client I'll be cooking for tomorrow because I'm not about to go to the grocery store at six in the morning just to get out of going today.

On the positive side, if I'd stayed home like I wanted to, my eyes would be much puffier and redder from all the extra time being sad about Max. My busyness has also been keeping me from having to deal with what is by now surely two very stinky bags from camping. They're probably sitting in my bedroom, making the whole place smell like dirt and campfire. And possibly skunk.

When I finally pull into the parking lot at the inn late Monday afternoon, relief washes through me to finally be home.

I step into the lobby, my arms laden with bags of groceries and my equipment like I'm a pack mule, and I hear Addison and Bex talking in the gathering room to my left and Timini's sewing machine in the kitchen and dining room to my right. So Addison must've finished up with clients early.

I texted the three of them to give updates on Max's injuries, but I haven't given updates on my relationship with Max. Which is good, because if I had shared the news about me and Max at any time earlier today, things wouldn't have been pretty for my clients.

And by "things," I mean my face.

But it's good they're all here now because I don't want to tell the story three times. They all hear me come in and help to lighten my load by taking some of the bags into the kitchen. As I start putting the cold groceries into the fridge and the others into my zippered bags, Addison asks, "How is Max doing today?"

"I don't know, actually." My voice comes out quieter than I mean it to.

"Pey?" Bex says, prompting me for more information.

I put the cheese into the drawer, and then turn around to my friends and roommates. "Max says that he can't be a husband or a dad, so things can't work out between us. I already knew he felt that way, but it still hurts to hear it. So he thinks we should stop dating."

"Oh, Peyton," Addison says, and all three women come in for a group hug.

With my arms around them, I lay my head on Timini's shoulder. The flowing tears finally stopped sometime during the middle of the night, but my body still manages to produce ugly hiccuping breath-hitches that sound suspiciously like sobs.

"Why did I have to kiss him at the wedding?" I ask them, not really expecting an answer. "Everything was just fine before, and then I went and ruined it all. I knew he didn't want a marriage and kids. See? This is why I shouldn't be trusted to make my own decisions! An eight-ball would be better at this than I am. In fact, I should go out and buy an eight-ball and start letting it do all my deciding. Then maybe I wouldn't be in messes like this."

"Well," Timini says as she tries to brush a tear off my cheek along with the lock of hair that was stuck to it from the tears and the hugging, "on the positive side, at least you won't have to worry about being Peyton Peyton. Or about Bex calling you Pey Pey."

I let out a sobbing chuckle. I don't see the looks on Addison's or Bex's face, but they must've shot Timini a look, because she very defensively says, "What? Peyton always looks on the positive side."

"Peyton," Addison says, and I lift my head from Timini's shoulder to look at her. "You're obviously good at decision-making."

I lift a skeptical eyebrow. Just because she says it doesn't make it true.

"Well, obviously you're good at it," Timini says. "Look at where you are. Look at who you are. Look at what you're doing. It was a lot of good decisions that got you to this point."

"No. I'm here because of luck and good advice."

Bex starts opening drawers, searching for something. "Where are sticky notes when you need them?" She finds a pad of them, then a pen, and motions all of us over to the dining table. "Okay, we're going to come up with a list of decisions you've made in your adult life."

I let out a breath and sit down. Bex looks like she's a woman on a mission, and it's pointless to try to stop her. "Okay, like what?"

Bex writes on the first piece of paper, "College," and then pulls it off the stack and sticks it to the table.

Ten minutes later, there's a huge pile of sticky notes that include everything from starting my own business to buying the cute floral blouse I'm wearing, to becoming friends with Max, to that time I cut my own bangs after my boyfriend broke up with me during my junior year of college, to moving into the inn, and everything in between. A good three dozen sticky notes are stuck in a cluster on the table.

Then Bex stands up and motions to her seat. "Sit. Look at each decision. If it turned out to be a good one, put it on the right. Bad ones go on the left."

As I go through the list, I'm surprised at how many sticky notes go on the right. In fact, the only ones on the left are relatively inconsequential. Like forgetting to make sure my back windows weren't down a crack before going through the car wash. (The inside of my car needed a good washing, anyway.)

And choosing not to check to make sure the quart of olive oil in my trunk has the lid screwed on tightly before I bring it in the house, along with armfuls of other supplies, because I was in a hurry. (For months, my old apartment looked better with shiny tile.)

And watching an infomercial that time I tried to skip an entire night's worth of sleep, just to see if I could do it. (Who doesn't want a supply of Snuggies, the wearable blanket, in every color ever made?)

By the time I'm done, I'm in shock at how many are on the "Good choices" side. Probably more than three-fourths.

"See?" Addison says, motioning at the sticky notes like she's Vanna White. "You always listen to your gut and think things through. You should trust your ability to make good decisions more."

"And you've stayed friends with Max for four years," Timini says. "You listened to your gut in becoming friends with him, and you've loved that decision."

I look from my friends to the sticky notes on the table. "Becoming friends was a good decision. But deciding to turn it into a romantic relationship wasn't."

"Listen up, Pey." Bex grabs hold of my hands like she wants to be able to just zoom the info from her head to me through our hands. "You said that when everything changed at the wedding, it was because David had opened the flood-gates, right?"

I nod. "That was the problem. That was why I made the bad choice."

"Nope. Not a bad choice. Your gut had been feeding you information on the right decision for years, and you'd just been shoving it all behind those gates. So when he opened the gates, all those thoughts and feelings that spilled out were your gut helping you to decide. It told you to go for that relationship. It wasn't a spur-of-the-moment thing. That answer had been percolating for years."

"Think back to the wedding," Timini says. "Imagine you never kissed Max. You never did anything to start that rela-tionship moving forward. How would you feel now?"

I imagine that scenario, and wow. I had not expected that *not* kissing him would feel so wrong. Not for a second would I have skipped these past few weeks with Max as a boyfriend instead of just a best friend.

"This," Addison says, motioning to the little yellow notes, "proves that you listen to your gut and make good decisions, even when someone isn't making them for you. And since you are a good decision-maker, then the fact that you opened yourself to a relationship with Max means that in your gut, you have hope that things will work out. You need to trust that."

I realize that I do have hope that things with Max will still work out. And that maybe my dad and my roomies have been right about my ability to make my own decisions. I do trust my own gut. And that causes a bubble of excitement to build up in my chest that makes me want to take action. I just need to figure out what that action should be.

# CHAPTER 25
## *Max*

WHEN I HEAR the knock on my apartment door, I hurry to it as quickly as a body that recently got slammed into a rock face can, hoping it might be Peyton, here to call me on my poor choices and make everything better. Not that she can fix any of my issues other than the ache I feel for her. When I open it, though, Hunter is standing there instead.

As my friend walks in, I ask, "How's Tami?"

"She's home. Physically, she's doing as well as could be expected. Emotionally?" Hunter shrugs. "It's hard. She's resting now. She told me I should come and check on you, and it looks like a good thing I am. Are you sure you shouldn't still be in the hospital? You look awful."

I sit in the padded chair that I've discovered has armrests at the perfect height for my sling, and Hunter sits on my couch. "I ended things with Peyton last night. Well, I ended the dating part. I'm hoping the friendship part can survive, but I don't know. I don't know if we can go back to the way things were before now that we know what it's like…"

I can't even finish the sentence. What it's like to date each other finally? What it's like to hold her in my arms? To kiss her? To be so much more than we ever were as friends?

Hunter's eyebrows rise, but then he looks down, like the fact that I ended things doesn't surprise him yet it explains why I look so awful. "Because the camping trip didn't go well and so now you think you can't get married?"

It sounds so stupid when he lays it out like that. "You've got to admit: it went bad." I tick off the items on my fingers. "Flat tire, skunk, raccoons, squirrels, my injury, Tami's miscarriage. That many things going wrong during one trip, the only one I've ever done with Peyton, is a pretty convincing sign that it's not going to work out." I feel bad, wallowing in my own struggles when Hunter is hurting, too.

Hunter is quiet for a long moment. Then he says, "You know it's not about the camping, right? It was never about camping. It's about your relationship with your dad and your thoughts about your parents' relationship."

I look at where the scrapbook my mom gave me is sitting on the coffee table.

"Maybe it's even about your relationship with Laurel." Hunter lets out a long breath. "I don't think I need to say anything about how great you and Peyton are together. I think every single cell in your body knows that. What I do think you need to do is realize that you are responsible for everything in your life. And not just responsible for it, but capable of changing it. Want a life with Peyton? Figure out your issues. Change your situation."

Ouch.

It's not like Hunter is telling me anything I don't already know at some level. It's not even the first time Hunter has told me that. It hurts worse this time, though.

After Hunter leaves, I pick up the scrapbook my mom gave me. She made it for me to relive happy memories, so how bad can it be?

As I flip through the pages and pages of pictures, I do come across a lot of happy memories. Birthday parties, racing down the street on bikes with my friends, school awards, scout pins earned, looking proud in my first suit, lots of different sports activities, my first time riding a horse, building a bonfire in my backyard, standing next to the hole I dug in my backyard that I'd thought was big enough to be a swimming pool.

But flipping through them also makes me realize how many of those pictures were taken by babysitters, neighbors, a friend's parent, teachers, scout leaders, or friends. There are hardly any pictures with either of my parents in them. It's not just because one of them was behind the camera, either. They simply weren't present at any of those picture-worthy moments.

And in the pictures where they are present, it's always both of them, and they always have the same smiles. The ones that aren't real—they're the "See? We can pull off the happy family image long enough to snap a picture" smiles that my parents were famous for.

I knew my dad had been absent most of my life. Somehow, I'd forgotten how absent my mom had been. Maybe because after the divorce when I was in junior high, she was around more but my dad was around even less, which was saying something.

And just like that, all the sadness and loneliness I had as a kid comes back, full force. I don't think any parent should ever be as absent in their child's life as mine were. I vowed back when I was in fifth grade that I would never be a dad like my dad was. And that I'd never have a marriage like my parents'. But seeing all of these pictures doesn't help. They all feel like proof that I came from two people who weren't good at being parents or spouses.

The pictures continue after my high school graduation, which surprises me. When I come across some of my father's viewing and burial, instead of pushing my emotions away like I usually do, I let myself feel them. All of the regrets, all the pain of my dad abandoning me permanently, all the sadness at missed opportunities, all the anger about not feeling like I had a dad.

Then I come across two pictures I've never seen. One is of Peyton hugging my mom at the burial, and one is her holding my hand as I stand in front of the casket, giving my dad a final goodbye. I had only been friends with Peyton for a few months at that point, but she helped me get through those first weeks after my dad passed. It was the thing that strengthened our friendship so quickly.

As I look at the picture of her hugging my mom, I realize how much she has done to help me improve my relationship with my mom. We hadn't been close at all before Peyton came along, and if it wasn't for her, I probably still wouldn't have much of a relationship with her.

It makes me wish I'd known Peyton for longer. Long

enough that she could've helped me improve my relationship with my dad because even though I never trusted him to be around, I realize that I wish I'd spent more time with him. Because now, I can't go talk to him. I can't ask him what I need to know.

Before I even have time to think about it, my phone is in my hand and I'm calling my mom. She answers and starts in with the small talk, but my mind is too full for that. I need my questions answered. "Mom. Why was Dad absent so much of the time?"

As my mom takes a deep breath, I hold mine. I expect her to say, "He just wasn't dad material. Not everyone is," because that's my biggest fear about myself.

Instead, she says, "I ran into Judy about a year ago."

"Dad's ex-wife?" I don't know her well at all. I haven't thought about her in a long time.

"Yeah. We talked for quite a while. It was nice, actually. And we talked about your dad, so I know exactly what your dad would say if you asked him that question. He would say, 'Every single day, you choose to put your focus on what is most important to you. It's a conscious choice.' And he would also tell you that he made the wrong choice."

The words hit me with a physical force that makes me fall back into my chair, reminding me of just how injured I am. "You think he wished he would've been around more?"

"I think it was his biggest regret that he constantly made the wrong choice." She's quiet for a long moment and then says, almost in a whisper, "I *know* he wished he would have been around more because I wish I would've been, too. I have those same regrets, those same wishes that I would've spent more time with you.

"Then Peyton came along. She got me to recognize my mistakes. She helped me to turn things around while I still have the chance, and I'll be forever grateful for that girl."I sit, too stunned to talk.

"She taught me that it's never too late to make different choices. I'm betting she's taught you the same thing."

"Why didn't you tell me this before?"

"You haven't always been in a place where you could handle hearing how your dad felt. I was waiting for you to be ready."

"I know I don't tell you this often, but you're a good mom. Thank you."

My mom sucks in a quick breath. After several long moments, her next words come out filled with emotion. "I love you, son."

"I love you, too," I say, and I do.

I hang up the phone, feeling a mix of sadness and heaviness about a past I wish I could change and a lightness greater than I can ever remember experiencing about a future that I *can* change. I haven't allowed myself to believe before this moment that being a good husband and eventually a good dad doesn't have anything to do with my genes. It's all a choice and not something outside of my control.

Even the way my relationship with Laurel went was a choice. I bickered right back, and I chose to stay in that relationship for so long because I thought it was exactly what was to be expected.

Peyton helped me realize long ago that I don't want to be that person, and it's been a long time since I have been. And I decided long before I knew her what kind of dad and husband I wanted to be. I just need to let go of those past fears that I've been holding onto so tightly.

Now is the time to be the man I've always wanted to be.

# CHAPTER 26

*Peyton*

"CAKE!" I say as I open the cupboard where we keep the mixing bowls. "I should make a fortress cake. Because it feels like our relationship grew into a fortress. Then I could take it to Max and say something about how our fortress can't be toppled so easily and that we need to defend it. Except cake isn't really very fortress-like. Hmm." I try thinking of a dessert that is more dense. Like stone.

"Or," Timini says, "you could just text him."

I think for a minute and decide texting would probably work just as well. Besides, no dessert that's dense like stone sounds good. So I pull out my phone and type out a text. *Hi. Are you home? I want to come over and talk.* I backspace over the *and talk* part because I don't want to sound scary. Then I imagine him reading it and thinking it sounds like I'm trying to pretend like our breakup didn't happen, so I delete all of it. After hesitating a few moments, trying to think of what to say, I just type *Can I come over?* and then press send before I can second-guess it.

There. Done. It's vague, so he can interpret it however he wants to. Except I'm suddenly unsure if that's a good thing. I hold my breath, waiting for his response, my heart beating a million miles an hour.

A minute later, his response comes in.

> Max: Instead, can you meet me at Pioneer Park at nine? In that clearing on the north side of the pond. I need to pay up for losing our competition.

Tonight? While he's still recovering? I type *Max, you don't have to do it so soon* and press send.

> Max: Yes, I do. Will you meet me there?

Really, I would meet him anywhere.

> Peyton: Yes.

It's fully dark when I pull into the lot at Pioneer Park. From there, I can see the playground at the right, but trees hide the pond. I follow the winding trail off to the left that leads through the trees. Butterflies are having a party in my stomach, and the skin on my arms feels like it's on high alert, noticing even the slightest breeze. Even though it's not cold outside, I rub my arms to get them to calm down.

I know that the pond is small and there are a few lights

around it, but I still worry that I won't be able to see where Max is.

Once I'm past all the trees that have been blocking my view, I see the clearing at the north end of the pond and two strings of lights leading into the woods at the end of the clearing. I head toward them, and when I get closer, I see that a lamp sits on a little table. An envelope with *Peyton* written on it in Max's handwriting is tucked just under the edge of the lantern.

I open the envelope, and inside, a card reads *Follow the lights*. So I pick up the lantern and do just that. They lead down a natural pathway between the trees, the strings of lights guiding me. I've been to the pond plenty of times, but this is the first time I've headed off into the woods here. The cedars and Douglas firs towering over me remind me of going camping with Max. This place even has that same fresh, earthy smell. That feeling and that smell are so intrinsically tied to Max—I've missed it.

Eventually, the trail and the strings of lights through the woods open up into a dark clearing. I hold up my lantern but it doesn't shine enough light for me to see further than a few feet in front of me. I want to walk forward, into the unknown, but nerves flutter in my stomach. "Max?" I call out.

Another set of lights turns on, bathing the clearing in golden light and showing that the space contains an actual couch. Just like one in a regular house, but sitting on the pine needle-covered ground. A little table is nestled in front of it, and across from it in the clearing sits a big outdoor movie screen. "Oh my lands," I say out loud. Is Max going to sing his karaoke song to a video? Maybe it will be the music video for whatever song he chooses.

Whatever it is, I love the idea. I love the couch, the screen, and the woods that are right in town but feel exactly like camping. He's gone to a lot of work to set this up. Maybe it's because even though he doesn't want to date anymore, he wants to try to make sure our friendship can stay intact. I like that it means this much to him.

And I want the friendship, too. But I also want more. I want it all, and I want it with Max. I know it to my core now, and no matter where that leads us—even if it leads me to heartbreak—I trust myself in making that decision more than any I've made in my life.

I walk over to the couch and sit down. That's when I notice a remote control on the table with a sign on it that reads *Press play*. So I do.

The projector on the table hums to life, and the big outdoor screen lights up with a photo—a selfie Max took of the two of us eating cotton candy at the Quicksand Carnival a couple of years ago. Music plays in the background of the video as it switches to a five-second clip of the two of us at a get-together with friends at Christmastime. Then a picture of us in a theater before the movie starts.

The video shows pictures and video clips one after another of so many things we've done together over the past four years. Some make me laugh, some bring a tear to my eye, and some have me grinning like it's my birthday. Some of the pictures are of things I haven't thought about in years. Some I've seen before and some are new. Seeing the past four years of our life together in one place like this makes all the emotions I feel about Max swell up and overflow. I wipe away a tear that has escaped.

Then a picture comes up in the video and it stays on the screen. It was taken just over a week ago as Max and I walked down the sidewalk in front of the shops on Settler's Boulevard, heading nowhere in particular, just enjoying being together. I had stopped to take a selfie with him, but a stranger had offered to take the picture for us.

I have stared at it several times since then just to relive the feelings of that moment. Max's arm is around my back, and we're both looking at each other like we couldn't be more in love. Max's face is especially adorable in the picture, and I stare at it now.

Then the song on the video changes to *Marry You*, and I gasp.

No. That can't be the reason why he chose that song. He just chose it because it has a great tune. This isn't about that.

Then Max steps out from behind the big screen and starts to sing. The lyrics aren't the same as they are in the song, though. He sings about how we have been friends for so long and how great that has been. He doesn't have perfect pitch, or anything close to it. But he has confidence, and that is even more attractive. The man looks like a dream.

He may have an arm in a sling, but he is moving as though he doesn't hurt, unlike the last time I saw him. And the words he is singing are just so sweet.

"Hey, Peyton," Max sings, "I think I am in love with you."

Max and I love each other. We have for a long time—this isn't new information. Max and I couldn't have been as good of friends as we are without loving each other. Being *in love*, though, is something completely different, and his words make my heart blow up like a balloon.

Then Bex, Addison, and Timini all step out from behind the screen and start being Max's backup singers, dancing to the music, and I scream and clap. How are they in on this without me having a clue?

Max sings the next verse, matching the music pretty impressively, but changing the lyrics to be about how I tried to kiss him a year ago and how he'd been in love with me even back then. *He had?* And about how he'd been so scared at the time and said something he had regretted so many times. He makes a face that has me laughing out loud.

Then his friends, Hunter, Emilio, and Leo, all come out from behind the screen and join Addison, Bex, and Timini as the backup singers. I find myself grinning until my cheeks hurt as I sway to the music.

When Max starts singing about when I kissed him in the moonlight, I blush and goosebumps run down my arms. I had been so nervous that night. Now I realize it was one of the bravest things I've ever done, and I am so glad I did.

Ian and Roman join the others in front of the screen that shows Max and me being in love, and I shake my head. He has lined up all of this for me. I want to jump out of my seat and hug him. But I also want this moment to never end, so I am not about to do anything to cut it short.

"Guess what, Peyton," Max sings, his eyes on mine, making me feel like I am the most important person in his universe. "I know I am in love with you."

My heart starts sprinting. And then it keeps on sprinting

when my dad and Max's mom also appear and join everyone singing. How have all of them been back there without me suspecting it? Or hearing them? I haven't fully recovered from Max's words before he goes on, singing about how we started dating and that since then, everything in the world has felt the most right. It is like he is singing exactly what my heart is feeling.

Everyone—Max, my five roommates, his three friends, my dad, and his mom—sings the next part of the song together, belting it out in the woods. When it gets to the part of the song that gives it its title, everyone stops singing and silently takes a few steps back toward the screen as the music fades to a soft sound.

Except Max. Max steps forward, coming right up to where I sit on the couch, and I want to leap up and wrap my arms around him. He pulls a ring box out of his pocket and then gets down on one knee. "Peyton…"

My hand flies to my mouth and before I know it, I am kneeling on the ground in front of him. "Max, yes! The answer is yes!"

He smiles, then reaches out and runs a knuckle along my cheek. "I haven't even asked the question yet."

My whole body is acting as if he has, though, including the tears that are falling. "It doesn't matter—the answer is yes. No, never mind. Ask. I need to hear the words or I'm not going to believe it. And if they aren't the ones you're making me think they are, Max, I will personally go out and find a startled skunk to bring back to you."

He laughs, and the sound is magical.

"Peyton. I'm not sure when the moment was that I first

fell in love with you, but I can tell you it was nearly four years ago. I'm sorry it took me so long to figure everything out that I needed to."

He gives me a smile that is sweet and so full of love and everything Max is, wrapped up into one little package. "We've been through practically everything together. When I think about the rest of my life, I know I want to experience everything it has to offer alongside you. And not only as my best friend but also as my wife." His voice is not shaky or unsure. It comes out with the confidence of someone who knows with exact certainty what he wants.

My breath hitches, and the tears are falling in earnest now.

"Peyton Abernathy, will you marry me?"

This time, I don't hold back. I wrap my arms around his neck and squeeze him tight, planting kisses all over his cheeks, saying "Yes" in between each one. The ten people watching—who I managed to forget all about the moment Max got on one knee—start cheering. Max and I are both smiling so wide we can barely kiss.

He stands and pulls me to my feet, then he wraps those strong, protective arms around me and pulls me close, and it feels like a promise that he will always protect my heart. He kisses my neck and then the space just under my ear, and then whispers, "I am in love with you, Peyton. And I want nothing more than to spend forever with you."

# CHAPTER 27
## Max

I LOVE that all our friends and family came to participate in my proposal. I also love that they know to leave not long after. Peyton has said yes, and I want to soak that in for as long as I can.

The two of us, alone in the clearing, sit on the couch. A part of me wants her to sit snuggled up into me so I can put an arm around her and she can lay her head on my shoulder. But the bigger part wants exactly what happens—Peyton sits facing me, her feet curled up under her, the strings of lights bathing her face in a golden glow. I sit with one leg bent in front of me, facing her, too, and I just take in how beautiful her eyes are. Her soft pink cheeks. Her perfect lips. Her golden curls.

"I'm really glad you're the one who lost our competition."

I laugh a hearty laugh. "Oh yeah?"

"Yep," she says, her lips curving into a smile. "I think you might have a future in karaoke."

"Maybe, but I am only going on tour with the show if we can sing as a couple. Oh! We can get business cards made up with our faces on them, holding microphones. Maybe even have a neighbor on it, too, knocking on the door to see if our cat is ill. And then it can go up on your office wall along with the rest of your business card collection in whatever house we live in."

This time Peyton laughs. Then her face turns more serious, and she runs a finger along one of the swirly designs on the sofa, biting her lip. "Max," she starts and then pauses. She opens her mouth to speak again and then closes it.

So I reach out with my good arm and hold her hand in mine, giving it an encouraging squeeze.

Peyton takes a breath, and then says, "Did you propose because you *want* to get married? Or only because you know it's what I want?"

"I *thought* I didn't want marriage. Or a family. It turns out I had an emptiness right here—" I reach up and touch my chest, right over my heart "—that was trying to tell me I was wrong. I had just lived with it for so long that I didn't fully know it was there. If it weren't for you, I would still be thinking it was normal—a flaw in the way I was made." I can't believe I am actually admitting this stuff out loud. If it was anyone other than Peyton, I wouldn't.

"The thought of living a life without you is probably the only thing that could've made me search out the source of that hole and work my way through it."

Peyton gives me that smile of hers that feels like it can power the sun. "And you did work through it?"

I nod. "That's how I knew that you fit perfectly into the space like it was made for you."

She reaches out and puts her hand over my heart. "I like being here."

I put my hand over hers, holding it there. "There's nothing I want more than to be able to spend the rest of my life married to you, Peyton. I wish I would've figured things out sooner because I don't want to waste a moment."

"That's just what my dad said." When I raise an eyebrow in question, she adds, "After his heart attack—the real one—he told me that he wanted me to get out and find the person I was supposed to spend my life with. And he said, 'Don't waste any of the years you could have together.'"

"That might have been why his smile was so big when I told him I wanted to propose to you."

Peyton chuckles.

"I wish you could've seen the smile on my mom's face, too, when I told her."

Peyton grins like everything in the world is perfect, and then she snuggles into me. I wrap the arm not in a sling around her, knowing she is exactly right.

I **PUT** a tablespoon of sesame oil in the pan on the stove, just like the recipe says, and then spread it around with the spatula before dumping the cut-up veggies in. It's my turn to cook for the roommate dinner, and I found a recipe online for 15-minute Lo Mein that looked easy.

Except the recipe lies. It took me thirty minutes just to cut up all of the carrots and green onions and cabbage and mushrooms and red peppers, especially since I keep getting distracted by thoughts of a pirate costume I'm designing. And then it takes a few minutes longer because I don't think to cook the lo mein noodles while I'm cutting up vegetables.

But I already have the soy sauce, sesame oil, and sugar for the sauce whisked up in a bowl, and am feeling pretty proud of myself for getting all the ingredients ready to go into the pan before I put the first ones in. I'm getting better at this cooking thing.

But suddenly, I'm wondering how frequent the "stir" is supposed to be in "stir fry."

At least this is an original roommates' dinner instead of the one with significant others. Cooking for four is less pressure than cooking for seven.

Peyton comes running into the kitchen, her curls bouncing, and her face flushed. "Guess what?"

Addison and Bex both stop setting the table and look up.

I give the vegetables another stir. "Um…You found a venue, set a wedding date, and it's only three months away."

"How did you know?"

"Wait." I look around. "I was right?"

"We decided that since we both have small families, we could totally do a wedding on the beach. We found the most beautiful spot with the most adorable place for the wedding dinner—and the ceremony, if it rains that day. It's perfect." She places some brochures down on the table. "And they had a cancellation, so a date was available. We just really don't want to waste any time in getting to our together life, you know? And three months—well, two and a half, actually—to plan a wedding isn't crazy. Right?"

All three of us join Peyton in a group hug, squealing.

"That's plenty of time to plan a wedding," I say.

Bex looks like she isn't so sure, but she still smiles and says, "Right. And we'll help."

Peyton lets out another squeal. "Two and a half months and I'll be Peyton Peyton!"

As we all gather around the brochures to look at the venue, Peyton says, "We were going to look for places to live, but, well, I wanted to talk to you all. Addison, since Ian lives here, and Bex, since you and Roman are going to be here for another four or five months—"

"Six months," Bex cuts in. "The builder ran into some problems and had to delay our move-in date."

"Oh. I'm sorry."

Bex waves her off. "It's fine."

"Well, and since Bex and Roman will be here for six months, Max and I kind of want to join in on the fun for as long as we can. You know, keep us all together for a bit longer. How would you all feel about Max moving in after the wedding?"

"Oh, whew," I say. "Now I don't have to enact my elaborate plan to keep you here longer."

Peyton laughs, but the truth is, I've actually been coming up with plans. I'm used to spending a good half of my workdays in the same room as Peyton, and I'm going to miss her terribly when she moves out.

"I think him moving in is perfect," Addison says. Then she sniffs. "What's that smell?"

The smell hits my nose at about the same time. Panicked, I rush around to the stove on the island counter and grab the spatula. The more I "stir" the stir fry, the more I see how many of the bottom parts of the vegetables are burned black.

The recipe says to put in a couple tablespoons of mirin—a mysterious clear liquid that is who knows what—to loosen the browned bits in the pan. So I splash the liquid in the pan and stir some more. It does help to loosen the browned—black, actually—bits, but it just spreads the black bits to the few parts of the veggies that aren't already blackened.

Bex looks into the pan and then at her wrist, even though she isn't wearing a watch. "Time of death: seven-thirteen."

I move the pan off the heat and pull out my phone. "And, we're having take-out for dinner! It's my specialty, anyway."

"No need," Bex says, opening the fridge and pulling open a drawer. "I'm sure we have enough random veggies in here. We can cut some up in no time. It'd be a shame to waste those noodles and that sauce."

As Bex and I cut up more vegetables and Peyton talks more about her upcoming wedding, my mind starts wandering in the direction of dating. I don't need a man to complete me. I never have. I've always been just fine on my own.

Except lately, I've been thinking about how nice it would be to have someone. Someone serious. It's been a while since I've been in a committed relationship. And it's definitely not because lately I've been surrounded by couples in love who've completely ignored our pact not to fall in love. It has nothing to do with that at all.

In fact, you know what? I'm fine. I don't need someone serious. There is nothing wrong with dating guys who are beautiful but shallow and having things end after a date or two. They are the ones I always seem to pick, and who doesn't like going with their default choice? There's a reason why established patterns hang around for so long. They're classic. They have staying power.

Well, okay, and they're boring and predictable and produce the same results.

"Oh, Timini," Bex says. "I forgot to tell you. Remember

how you told Roman that his company should make a dating app where you can't see each other's pictures, so you have to rely solely on the conversation the two of you strike up to see if you're a good fit? They are making it!"

I perk up. "For real?" I've always thought I might make better decisions on who to date if I couldn't just choose the ones with the prettiest faces.

"Yep," Bex says, grinning. "It'll be ready for beta testers soon, and Roman is hoping you'll be one of the first to try it out and see how you like it."

I smile. Maybe it's time to toss away boring and predictable after all. New and different? That is exactly what I need.

––––––––

Author's note:

I hope that as you read Peyton's and Max's story, you spent equal amounts of time happy sighing and laughing! And that you loved being back at the Hidden Inn with this group of friends. The only roommate left who hasn't broken the pact to not fall in love is the one who had taken it most seriously—Timini.

If you're a fan of witty banter, especially over text, then I think you're going to love the story of her and Jackson finding their happily ever after. Keep reading for a short sneak peek from one of Jackson's first chapters.

–Meg

———

I've just parked in my reserved spot in the parking garage for my building and am heading to the lobby when my little sister, Emma, calls.

"Are you home?"

"In the building."

"Great. I'm coming over to help you with your dating profile."

"Wait!" I head toward the mailboxes, where several other residents are picking up theirs, too. "Don't come. I'm having second thoughts."

"Not allowed. You already made this decision."

"Is now really the time, though? I'm leaving for Delhi in a day and a half, and I'm going to be gone for three weeks."

"That's not the reason you're stalling."

I curse under my breath. Emma and Ethan have the whole *I'm your twin so I can read your mind* thing going on. But I swear that Emma can use it on everyone, not just Ethan. Or at least everyone in our family. It makes it hard to do things like lie about the true reason I'm getting cold feet in regards to a dating app.

I put my key into my box, open it, and pull out the half a dozen envelopes inside. "It sounded like a good idea when I was talking with Roman about it. I was even on board earlier today. But, I don't know. Now I'm not so sure."

"Why." It is not a question—it is a demand. For most of my life, I have fought Emma on her demands. She is the youngest and I am the oldest, so if anyone is the boss of anyone, she isn't the boss of me. But she is relentless on some things, and it sounds like this is one of them.

I heave out a long breath. "Because it feels like admitting defeat."

"Explain."

"Dating apps are for people who can't get dates on their own." I'm not about to admit that not being able to get dates on my own means I have lost the ability. I'm kind of worried that maybe I have, but I'm nowhere close to being ready to full-on admit it.

"No," Emma says, dragging out the word, "they're for people who aren't meeting people to date in their normal routines. You aren't meeting the types of people you want to date doing what you're doing, so you need to do something different."

"Maybe." The types of people I do meet are very much not the type I want to be in a relationship with. "But it's also a lot of work setting everything up, chatting with a ton of people to narrow it down to who I should date, and going on lots of dates to find someone with relationship potential."

"And you're afraid that if you fail using a method of finding dates that you already see as second-class, it'll make you feel like a loser."

"What? No, I'm not afraid."

"Then do it."

She is goading me. Earlier, it was worth it to give in to her need to be the boss. Now it isn't. "Not going to happen."

"You'd rather die alone, after a life spent in unfulfilling relationships."

Of course, I wouldn't. "Sounds good. Sign me up for the unfulfilling life."

"You are impossible."

Get *How to Not Fall for Your Ex* and read Jackson's and Timini's story

**Twelve years ago, he broke my heart. Now I'm falling for him all over again—one anonymous message at a time.**

I don't see a point in dating. Relationships are messy and they never end well. Plus, there's the part where I seem to pick guys who are only pretty on the outside.

So when a friend asks me to beta test a new blind dating app —the kind where you *can't* see photos—I say yes, figuring I'll spend a week chatting with strangers and confirming that dating is still the worst.

Except… I really like one of the guys I'm messaging. He's smart, funny, surprisingly sweet, the absolute best at flirty banter, and is my opposite in the best way. His name's Jackson, and against all odds, I'm catching actual feelings.

There's just one problem.

When we finally meet in person, I find out that Jackson is Jack Oliver—*my* Jack. My high school boyfriend. The one who went from perfect to pretentious faster than you can say "family money." The one who ripped my heart out.

Now I don't know if the guy I've been falling for is real… or just another version of the Jack who hurt me.

All I know is I'm *not* falling for my ex.
(Probably.)

*If you're a fan of witty text banter, second chances, and loads of chemistry and heart, you'll love* How to Not Fall for Your Ex.

**Start reading**

**Spies Don't Fall for Their Asset**
**Spies Don't Fall for Their Rival**
**Spies Don't Fall for Their Neighbor**

Meg Easton is the *USA Today* bestselling author of contemporary romances and romantic comedies with fun, memorable, swoon-worthy characters, and settings you'll want to pack up and move to. She lives at the foot of a mountain with her name on it (or at least one letter of her name) in Utah. She loves gardening, bike riding, baking, swimming before the sun rises, and spending time with her husband and three kids.

She can be found online at www.megeaston.com

Sign up to receive her newsletter and stay up to date with new releases, get exclusive bonus content, and more.

If you liked this book please leave a review. Your review can help other readers find books they might fall in love with.

- youtube.com/@megeastonauthor
- bookbub.com/authors/meg-easton
- instagram.com/megeaston_author
- facebook.com/MegEastonBooks
- tiktok.com/@megeaston_author